lury.gibson was founded in 1999. This is their first production.

Dangerous Data
LURY.GIBSON

BANTAM PRESS

LONDON · NEW YORK · TORONTO · SYDNEY · AUCKLAND

TRANSWORLD PUBLISHERS
61–63 Uxbridge Road, London W5 5SA
a division of The Random House Group Ltd

RANDOM HOUSE AUSTRALIA (PTY) LTD
20 Alfred Street, Milsons Point, Sydney,
New South Wales 2061, Australia

RANDOM HOUSE NEW ZEALAND LTD
18 Poland Road, Glenfield, Auckland 10, New Zealand

RANDOM HOUSE SOUTH AFRICA (PTY) LTD
Endulini, 5a Jubilee Road, Parktown 2193, South Africa

Published 2001 by Bantam Press
a division of Transworld Publishers

A catalogue record for this book is available from the British Library.
ISBN 0593 047419

Typeset in Optima/Zurich by Falcon Oast Graphic Art Ltd

Printed in Great Britain
by Clays Ltd, St Ives plc

1 3 5 7 9 10 8 6 4 2

ACKNOWLEDGEMENTS

With this book many of the Dogg's secrets are revealed. Nevertheless the Dogg is cool about publication. 'Information wants to be free,' and the escape committee who have encouraged, cajoled and advised the Dogg are thanked: Stephen Johnson, Quentin Baer, Gerrard Tyrell, David Newbury, Justin Turner and Liz Moor. The transformation of a collection of rambling case notes into a story was greatly aided by Sara Hoffbrand, Brian Cooper, Guy Rooney, Robert Bevan and Clive Holt-Bailey. And the realization of that story in print could not have happened without Julian Alexander, Peta Nightingale, Bill Scott-Kerr and all the switched-on team at Transworld. Finally, special thanks to Lyndall Gibson and Claire Crocker who inspired the Dogg to write and whose confidence was never shaken.

Card and Cheques

PERSONAL DATA

16.4 In processing Transactions, we may incidentally collect some limited personal data about your racial or ethnic origin, political opinions, religious or other similar beliefs, trade union membership, physical or mental health, sexual life or criminal record. You agree that we may use, disclose or transfer those personal data as described in this condition.

The name is Dogg. Arthur Dogg. Arthur C. Dogg to be exact. Special Investigator. Private Dick in a world without privacy. First generation Data Sleuth.

I am the new breed of detective. I don't stake out motels or tail cars or even tap phones. I deal in data. The stuff that people generate simply by living. Each time you use a credit card or take out a subscription to a magazine you create personal data. And the truth is, this data doesn't just get stored; it's sold, transferred, mined. Your private life is open for business.

If someone like me bothers, we can find out anything we want to know about you. It's waiting there on someone's database. Where you live, what you eat, where you go, what you earn. Every move you've ever made has left a clear little footprint in the white electronic sands. Tides turn, winds blow, day becomes night, but the footprints never fade. Nothing about you is ever lost. It's there, eternally retrievable. All we have to do is start looking.

Until recently I worked as part of a sifting team, investigating suspicious individuals. Now I work for myself. For anyone who pays, mostly corporations and the press.

That morning I was on a runner case for a bank. Tracing a certain Mr Philips who seems to have conveniently left his usual abode and would rather not be found at his new one. I was getting on well. Mr Philips was now Mr Evans and living in Newport: 32 Mount Drive. My clients would arrange a visit.

Then I get this e-mail.

> Garden Flat, 81 Bryanston Road, London NW6. Check it out.
> Sam Collier

That was all. The sender: samc@riverso.co.uk. Just an unassuming member of the public who needed my services. Not your usual contact, I admit. Private clients are often a bit edgy to start off. And the guy could have been a bit more informative about the job. But then that's e-mail for you. Shrink-wrapped vocabulary. The easier it is to communicate the less we have to say. No-one thinks they're Charles Dickens any more.

The Dogg
DATA DETECTIVE

<u>Looking for things you didn't know were there.</u>

thedogg@acdogg.co.uk

Like any profession, mine has its own code. It's simple: 'Keep the wolf from the door.' I work for money. So I send back an outline of my fees to this Mr Collier: £250 for the basic search – I call it the Home Truths package – £500 for missing persons, all other work on application. Not expensive, but it's the add-ons where I make my real money. Once they get a taste for it, customers always want more information.

I get the answer straight back.

> OK for Basic Search. Go ahead.

Confirmation is good enough for me. No upfront fees required. My clients rarely need reminding of their side of the bargain: the damage I can do to their credit files makes it far wiser to pay up. Besides, where are they going to hide?

And, I must admit, there was a certain poetry to Mr Collier's request.

One simple piece of data, that's all the Dogg has to go on. A house. It could have belonged to anyone. It could be a safe house, or a money drop, or a knocking shop. The Dogg is amazed sometimes at what goes on behind closed doors. You live in this quiet suburban street for years; then one morning the police cars arrive. Your neighbour gets bustled into the back of a wagon. You knew him, but you didn't know he ran a money-laundering business from his bathroom. That's the thing of it: you assume your neighbours are just like you. If you move into a new flat, you assume your flatmates are normal, fun-loving citizens. You want to think that way. It's mental insulation. Not knowing the truth about your neighbours or flatmates is the surest way to get to sleep at night.

I don't know my quarry. I don't need to. It could be anyone. It could have been you that I was asked to track. And I would have taken the job.

UK REGISTER OF ELECTORS

Address:
Garden Flat, 81 Bryanston Road
London NW6 8KR

1996
James Cameron
Robert Bolton

Waiting . . . more information . . .

Ronnie Reagan once said that you could tell a lot about a man by the way he ate his jellybeans. Well, Ronnie, these days an address can tell you much, much more. There's a whole big world of data logged to the hutch you inhabit.

That's why, for Dogg, the roof over your head doesn't keep the rain out. It keeps the data in. The walls soak up the facts. The front-door bell is hotsynched to an electronic key pad that stores your life. You are where you live.

You've always thought of home as rather comforting. Somewhere you feel safe, got all your things around you. But all those creature comforts are tagged with information. The telephone, the TV, the fridge and cooker, the sofa may all belong to you. But you don't own the information that goes with them. Think about it: your stereo plays music, but the details you filled out for that three-year warranty are filed on a remote database. Somebody else holds that information. And who's to say what they'll do with it?

I don't even need to get into your home to tell you what's inside, or where you bought your carpets, or how many payments are outstanding on the kitchen, or even what sort of lifestyle you lead. Your home is inside out.

And the access system is beautifully simple. I tap in to the electoral roll. Just a few seconds' wait. 81 Bryanston Road. Through the front door. Hello, James Cameron and Robert Bolton.

continued . . .

Address:
Garden Flat, 81 Bryanston Road
London NW6 8KR

1997
James Cameron
Robert Bolton

1999
James Cameron
Robert Bolton
Cynthia Shepherd

IS IT CONFIDENTIAL?
Yes, all the information we hold on our files complies with the Consumer Credit
Act 1974 and the Data Protection Act 1998.
   We only supply private information to bona fide enquirers who have a
genuine need for such information.

James and Robert aren't the only ones living at 81 Bryanston Road, London NW6 8KR. There's a Cynthia Shepherd under the same roof. She's a more recent addition.

James and Robert share the house for three whole years. Two mates, and then along comes Cynthia. Who did she know first? And was it a chance encounter, or work, or did they meet at some party? Conjecture, Dogg. For now, all we know is that there they are together, three characters in a house. At night they come home, swap tales and share the bathroom.

Yeah, that's right. The Garden Flat has one bathroom. And know what? Two bedrooms. As the Dogg often says: Three into two does go. The Age of Chivalry may be dead, but I bet Cynthia doesn't get the sofa.

So who sleeps alone? Or is there intrigue here? Do they share?

It's a New Day

This morning 25,000 people will sign up for a mobile phone service. 74 million people might hop on the Internet.

By noon, 450 million voice-mail messages will be left [not necessarily returned].

In the time it takes to say you'll be late for dinner, 5 million e-mails will be sent.

Lucent Technologies
We make the things that make communications work.

WALL STREET JOURNAL

The loss of privacy is the No. 1 concern of Americans as the 21st century approaches.

www.aclu.org/echelonwatch/faq.html

ECHELON is the term popularly used for an automated global interception and relay system operated by the intelligence agencies in five nations: the United States, the United Kingdom, Canada, Australia and New Zealand . . .

It has been suggested that ECHELON may intercept as many as 3 billion communications every day, including phone calls, e-mail messages, Internet downloads, satellite transmissions and so on. The ECHELON system gathers all of these transmissions indiscriminately, then distills the information that is most heavily desired through artificial intelligence programs.

I send an e-mail back to Mr Collier. Details of the names. The information my clients usually require. Pretty fast turnaround too – not bad for £250. I get a message back.

> Dogg
> Can't you do any better than that?
> Who are they?

Not the reply I expected. Not at all.

Who are James and Cynthia? Who is Robert? Seem easy enough questions, don't they? Well, you'd be wrong.

For instance, how I answer the question 'Who are James and Cynthia?' depends on the facts I discover; or, to be more accurate, on which facts are revealed, when. But James and Cynthia would answer this question very differently. Their response would be based on their internal story.

And the more I do this job the more I recognize that everyone has two answers to 'Who am I?' One internal and one external. The internal story is who you feel yourself to be. Maybe I should say the person you'd like yourself to be, since we all have a picture of ourselves that's relentlessly positive, full of hope and innocence. The internal story inhabits an edited world of partial views: everything filtered by justification, intimation, pride and prejudice.

The external story is the objective view, the data you have nailed to experience. It only deals with facts. No room for discussion. You did or you didn't do it? Right. That's my kind of story. In the Dogg's book, if you sell insurance, you're an insurance salesman. Now the insurance salesman, of course, may believe that he's really a poet. He's published no verse, but that's fine. He's the bard of his own internal voice. Which of us is right? Which story is true? The same person with two stories, told very differently.

thedogg@acdogg.co.uk

COOL LINKS

AOL NetFind
FIND A PERSON

USSearch.com

NetAddress:Login

www.mailbox.co.uk/esp ESP
E-MAIL SEARCH PROGRAM

www.iaf.net
INTERNET ADDRESS FINDER

rs/internic.net/cgi-bin/whois
WEB INTERFACE TO INTERNIC

worldemail.com
WORLD E-MAIL DIRECTORY

Who are they? The question is still bugging me. I can know anything. I can experience any subject: there are 1,247,340,000 sites just waiting for me. Downloading information in less than a second. But can I get to know people – who they are?

Who am I? I am Dogg. I chose the name, first because I need the anonymity; and second because on the Internet I can assume any identity I want, even a Dogg.

You don't know me. Because you don't have the data on me. And that's the way I like it. I am just an identity.

I reckon it won't be long until people start assuming new electronic identities, maybe even multiple IDs. They're already doing it in chat rooms all over the Internet. Why not conduct your whole on-line life as somebody else? I like to think of it as 'identity tourism'. Trying on new personalities, acting out different parts. All the world-wide web's a stage and we just click on our exits and our entrances. The theatre is a place called @. @ is not a physical space. It's an electronic dream. And @ doesn't locate you the person, it locates you the file. You the facts. You are where it's @.

We could even have parallel lives: electronic and active.

Right now I'm a detective. I am on a job. Mr C wants to know who these people are. So I have to mine the data into blocks, then I chisel the blocks. Like Michelangelo said in one of his sonnets about the art of sculpture: 'To break the marble spell is all the hand that serves the brain can do.' The marble spell. Data. Data is Carrara marble. You have to chip away at the block until you get down to the person inside. He or she is waiting to be discovered.

I mail Mr C.

> This is going to take time, Mr C. The price went up another £250.00.

And Mr C says:

> OK.

18/01/00 10.45

James File

James Alexander Cameron	b. Edinburgh 20/06/67
Nat. Ins. No.	TN670620Q
Nat. Health No.	861947753

Parents:

Richard Alexander Cameron	Actuary [d. 1991]
Alice Eliza MacKintosh	Secretary

2 brothers:

Alan Michael	b. Edinburgh 19/05/65
Francis Richard	b. Edinburgh 21/11/71

Graduated BA Hons Law Bristol University 1988 (First)

Qualified as Accountant	Arthur Andersen 1991
Current Employer	Arthur Andersen, Corporate Finance Accountant
Current Salary	£150,000.00
Defined Benefits	4 x salary life assurance
	Final salary scheme accruing 9/60 current £63,400.00 p.a.
	Andersen in-house AVC: £52,000.00 (UK Equity Growth)
Drives	BMW M5 V752FLF
Health Insurance	PPP WB 25918794F 4 claims
e-mail	jamesc@aandersen.co.uk
password	sophieeld
Credit Card	Lloyds Mcard
	4775 9180 2227 4176 Exp. 12/00

Last 5 Purchases

15/01	Austin Reed	£31.90 Menswear (2 x Jockey briefs)
14/01	BMW St John's Wood	£123.30 Service department
14/01	Odeon Cinemas	£16.00 Tickets Leicester Square
12/01	Dolland & Aitchison	£120.00 Contact lenses 6 months
08/01	Interflora	£30.00 Bouquet

James Alexander Cameron, born in Edinburgh, the middle brother. Parents well settled in Edinburgh. An honest family home. No need to move. Good schools for the kids and easy to get out at the weekends. James's mum, Alice, still lives there. What's more, James is doing well. Good job, good company. He runs a BMW.

Info is starting to come thick and fast. The thing is, it's the most insignificant piece that can give you the sweetest insight. So you have to accept what comes, sift and then interpret. In this case, my client just says: Who are they? So I have to start looking at data differently, building a personality around everyday signals.

For instance, James drives a BMW – so that tells me quite a bit about money, status, attitude to status and so on. But what about an apparently random fact like James wears Calvin Klein Jockey pants, would that help? Well, yes – because it helps you determine the stereotype. However snooty people get about the subject, there's nothing wrong with stereotypes. It's the mind's short cut; the place from which we build first images and then add personality as we go along.

BMW-driving, Jockey-sporting James – gets you thinking.

BMW AG   Credit Rating   --/--/A-1

Much of the current company success has stemmed from the development of the consistent marketing policy [the 'market niche' strategy]. The BMW brand has been built on the four core values of technology, quality, performance and exclusivity.

THE ULTIMATE BRIEF SURVEY
RESULTS

Guys, what kind of underwear do you wear?

Jockeys	49 %
Boxer briefs	19 %
Bikinis	18 %
Boxers	11 %
None	3 %

Here's what I like to do in my underwear (check all applicable)

Sleep	25 %
Lounge	23 %
Have sex	18 %
Exercise	11 %
Eat	9 %
Answer the door	6 %
Take Hermann to the circus	5 %

What colour do you wear most often?

White	58 %
Other	15 %
Blue	12 %
Grey	8 %
Red	3 %
Green	0 %
Yellow	0 %
Brown	0 %

BMW means enough CC to suggest he's successful, but not too much so he's showy. Sure, it's a status auto. But it's status quo. It's not about risk. Not a gambling man's machine. Well, not new anyway; although a different dynamic kicks in second hand. If it's a second-hand BMW, then it's all about wanting the lifestyle you don't have. And that's when you start to deal in gamblers. But for new-car buyers, it's a real driving machine; masterful engineering, the beauty of the thing that works.

The Jockeys? Let's just say that life divides males into boxer-boys, Y-fronters and those who don't wear anything at all. Much controversy surrounds the argument over which is better for your sex life. The Dogg is not much interested in this, because frankly it's just a ruse to gain editorial inches for men's underwear which are an otherwise rather unnewsworthy subject – unless they've been left somewhere indiscreet or taken off when they shouldn't have been.

But, Mr C, the CK brand label should be of interest to you. It says something about James. The brand he wants to wear next to his man-hood. And brands go right to the nub. Tell you about the general condition of mankind today. We are both influenced and owning. We believe brands can define us, because we want them to have meaning. We actually want them to be signs, signifiers, whether subtle or obvious. A means to a new identity, they answer 'Who am I?' with another question: 'Never mind who you are, who do you want to be?' You don't have to worry who you are, or what class you come from, or where you went to school. None of that matters. Be who you want to be, and change whenever it suits. That's why people are not just one brand. When it comes to the gear you wear, you can put on or take off different identities. Everyone is a bunch of inconsistencies. We're all a series of lifestyles in flux. That's how come we get fashion.

So is it unusual that the Dogg should put such store by brands? No. If you believe they define you, why shouldn't Dogg? Brands are facts. Use them to fill out the pattern.

James File

James Cameron

Scottish Provident Life Assurance Policy 13219867L

Non-Smoker

UK DIVORCE REGISTER

JAMES CAMERON – SOPHIE CAMERON [ELDRIDGE]
Decree Absolute granted this day 12th January 1994.

www.UK Health.com

% OF SMOKERS IN ENGLAND

1975	36
1980	34
1985	33
1990	31
1995	27

% OF SMOKERS WHO ARE MALE

1975	48
1995	32

70 % of smokers say they want to give up

50 % of 15–20 yr olds have experimented with some form of drugs

My initial search also turned up old university files, life policy, CV, company databank and so on. His life assurance tells us he is a lapsed smoker. He was a member of the Fabian Society at university, but doesn't seem to have taken politics any further. A youthful aberration. He has had his appendix removed; he also had a spell in hospital as a teenager – unclear as yet what for (the older records are a bit patchy). He seems sporty – played for the university second XV rugby team. He worked in the US during one long vacation. He speaks French. He was married at twenty-four. Divorced at twenty-six. Reason cited: her adultery. No children. He likes skiing; four trips in the last three years. He belongs to the National Trust.

Employers' records, CVs, insurance files, VISA card details: life laid out in neat little blocks. Chip away and the form emerges. You start to see James or Cynthia or Robert. You begin to answer 'Who are they?' Isn't that what happens in all stories? You build a world from the facts the storyteller chooses to share. But it's a mirage, because it's always the author's invention. The author has already decided how they want you to feel, so they give you the facts – and only those facts – that are in line with their story. I select facts. Of course. There'd be too much information otherwise. But I don't ignore facts. If something doesn't fit, I still have to work with it. My pattern is not all neat and tidy character-ization. There are elements that don't fit. That's the way I have always found people. Just when you think you've got to know someone they do something completely 'out of character'. Most people get confused by this – get outraged that their neat formula has proved untrue. And therefore they deny it: 'That can't be true, he just wouldn't do that,' they say. But I find it fascinating. It makes me question whether there is anything such as true character, but rather patterns of behaviour which may break down. Anyone is capable of anything.

This is a truer fiction. An electronic mirror held up to nature. Look in.

Check Out Your Date

Today dating has become even more complex than before. Finding someone to date can be as easy as looking in the 'dating' classifieds that most papers have, calling a dating hotline to meet someone, searching the Internet to find that someone special or asking out the waitress that serves you dinner! How do you really know that this person is someone special and not an axe-murderer? By the time you finish this article you will know at least a few basics so that you can check out any potential date before you even meet them face-to-face. Also, you will find a set of questions that you should ask yourself about this someone special. By knowing these things and doing a little homework, if and when you meet that person face-to-face for your first date you will know more about them.

What about love and romance? Why check out somebody when you just feel it is so right with them? Because your safety should always be your first concern.

CIBR Corporation

So far, James seems straightforward. Professional, stable (he wears Jockeys, right), and we know he's the marrying kind. He comes recommended with a solid family history. No broken homes to haunt the heart. For a female in search of a partner, I'd say he was a safe bet.

Of course, choosing partners is always a tricky affair. Most of us simply let it happen. You bump into someone through a mix of circumstance and chance, then you let the mechanics of the internal life take over. You build up a photo-fit image of the person you're with, based on who you want them to be. You never see the real person, because you don't want to. You're happier with approximations. So, when the facts change and things fall apart, you find you were with somebody else, somebody you hardly recognize. Sweet – the person closest to you becomes like some negative undeveloped. And all you have to say to them is: 'Maybe I never really knew you at all.'

Now, some people go searching for a partner. There's a whole big dating industry for those who prefer to start with the facts: *Blonde. Petite. GSOH. Non-smoker. Seeks fun-loving male.* Well, that sure narrows the field, doesn't it? You see, the trouble with amateurs is that they don't do enough spadework. They're not prepared to put in the hours. They make a gesture to the external story, to the facts. And they end up, always, wanting to be loved for 'who they really are', they want to be loved for the internal story. Of course, once you get into love, all sorts of things can cloud the vision. Passion, even in those least passionate, gets messy. It makes the murderer tender in the night. It drives the sensible mad.

18/01/00 11.05

Cynthia File

Cynthia Jane Shepherd	b. London 12/04/68
Nat. Ins. No.	TN8640910P
Nat. Health No.	247712685

Parents:

Gerald Arthur Shepherd	Potter
Rose Kenton	Florist

No siblings

Graduated BA Hons Anthropology Sussex University 1990 (2:2)

Current Employer	MORI Organization Associate Director
Current Salary	£52,000.00
Published Articles	<u>MORI Newsletter</u> 'The Conscience of Research' 09/98 'Research with Responsibility' 06/99
Market Research Society	Full Member
Drives	Peugeot 205 [Diesel] P242 XFX
Health Insurance	Norwich Union [3 claims – latest claim 06/98] CX5 982 784 LLP

Donates £50.00 per month to Rape Crisis Centre (under GAYE)

AA Member since 1992	AA Home Start
e-mail	cynths@mori.org
password	pr1vasee

Cynthia is cool. Anthropology degree. Suggests she's non-mainstream; does what she wants, not what she thinks others will approve of. A dreamer, an idealist. But *tendence* pragmatic: she drives a Peugeot. Member of the AA.

After she left university she travelled around for a year. Looks like she got jobs as she went; since there's no other obvious support line. She went to Latin America for four months and also to India for six weeks. All this is courtesy of government files. Governments are a godsend to Dogg. Ace source of facts; most of the work's already done.

Then Cynthia settles into a job. It's the responsible thing to do. And she's been there ever since. Obvious really, but the Peugeot is hers, not a company car. What's more, it's diesel. With that anthropology degree she's not going to monkey around with the planet more than she can help.

She works for MORI. Data world. Associate Director in the gathering and interpretation of facts. Except they're half facts. The big mistake they make is to try to turn opinions and feelings into facts. But opinions change with mood or information. Have you ever filled in one of those market research forms? They ask you to answer fifty questions in fifteen minutes. By the time you're halfway through you'll say anything! The interpretation is science, but the base data is flawed. Maybe that's why Cynthia feels she should justify her work – she writes a paper, 'Research with Responsibility'. You don't fool me. Responsibility indeed! You're trying to justify your methods, giving inner-world stuff a status it cannot have. Opinions aren't facts.

But here's a fact. And one which should interest you: Cynthia makes a regular donation to the Rape Crisis Centre.

18/01/00 11.10

Robert File

Robert James Bolton	b. Exeter 24/09/67
Nat. Ins. No.	TN0624476F
Nat. Health No.	746211459

Parents:

Julian Christopher Bolton	Lecturer [retd], now living with Henrietta Rogers [b. 12/03/61]
Maria Stephanie Cazenove	Lecturer, now living alone

1 sister:

Claire Maria	b. Exeter 18/02/72

1 brother:

Richard Stephen	b. 16/12/69; d. 12/04/94 [road accident]

Graduated BA Hons Sociology Bristol University 1988 [2:2]

Current Employer	Saatchi & Saatchi, Director
Current Salary	£120,000.00
TV Licence [paid]	
Drives	Audi TT Coupé T Quattro
Health Insurance	BUPA [no claims]
Personal Insurance	House contents [Guardian] value £20,000.00 [item: Rolex at £2000.00]
e-mail	robbo@saatchi-saatchi.com
	robbolton2@daemon.co.uk
password	latecopy
	loure8d

Robert James Bolton. Father was a lecturer, but Robert's gone for the money. A public school boy, though MPS – minor public school, that is. Works in advertising. Eldest child – one brother. Parents divorced. Dad's new partner is not much older than Robert.

He works for a big-name agency. Drives a car brand that's going places, taking over the niche of the 'independent' corporate mind: 'Yeah, I work for a company. But, like, I'm really my own man.'

Robert's brother died six years ago. Road accident. Robert owns a Rolex. Is it genuine or one of those perfect copies? Interesting, that: always the first question about a Rolex, is it genuine or fake? Does that mean we're always asking the same about the wearer?

Robert got a 2:2 Sociology degree; he was a member of the university drama club. He was fined £100 and penalized six points for driving without due care and attention four years ago. He belongs to the Chelsea Arts Club, but doesn't live in Chelsea. Member of Ronnie Scott's Jazz Club. He won a prize at the Edinburgh Festival at the age of twelve for poetry.

Getting to know you, James, Robert, Cynthia. Being led into the light.

INSTANT CV SEARCH
THE UK'S PRIMARY CV VERIFIERS

<u>Names searching:</u>
<u>Cynthia Shepherd</u>
<u>James Cameron</u>
<u>Robert Bolton</u>

Searching please wait . . .

Cynthia did well at school. Nine O levels, three A levels. She broke her leg when she was thirteen. Riding accident. She was a school prefect in a mixed school. Used to getting along with the boys from an early age; had to be as good as the boys at everything. Competitive, our Cynthia.

James was also a prefect. Robert was expelled. There's no explanation why – you know how secretive those minor public schools can be. Probably cannabis in the dorm. That's the usual story. Still, it didn't stop him doing well at A level; three straight As from the sixth-form college his parents sent him to after he had been kicked out. Smart and a bit of a black sheep, Robert. Things were never going to be easy for him. Something about Robert tells me he's not a safe bet – for the single female looking for a partner.

James File

Robert File

Bristol University Year Book 1987

GUNG HO CLUB

EST. 1987

The Gung Ho Club exists to promote adventure sports and daredevilry. Free spirits and raving lunatics only need apply. No 'tacks. No fear. No brains.

Hon. Sec.	Robert 'Woof Woof' Bolton
Treasurer	James 'Sniffer' Cameron
Members	David 'Pretty Boy' Leslie
	Andrew 'Lottie' Lomax
	Stewart 'Longhorn' Mackay
	James 'Tiger' Winton
	Tim 'Gunner' Bore
	Alex 'Slipper' Whetside
	Sophie 'Ganger' Green
	Tom 'Wolfman' Ellisson
	Amanda 'Randy' Allsop
	Chris 'The Belly' Flip

Robert and James met at university. Long-standing mates. They'd probably say they know everything about one another. But if you asked them for the lowdown, what you'd end up with is lots of inner life stuff. Things I do not need to know. Memories, nostalgia. Pub talk. An amusing story, anecdotes about various women, who shagged whom. But there would be few facts.

All the Dogg requires is facts. The rebel within is someone I never need to meet. He doesn't exist. Back in your box, James Dean. We all like to think we're rebels, that we've got this great free spirit roaming inside us and that if the chips were down we would be there on the barricades. But the facts don't support this. If you're not a rebel in fact, there's no rebel within. The water cannon would turn you back. Tear gas and Molotov cocktails are messages few will ignore.

Maybe the interesting thing about Robert and James is that they're still close friends after all this time: shows the bonding goes deep. And yet, although they've got interests in common, their patterns don't seem to fit. Like they both go for brunettes with small breasts – but one's a one-night-stand artist and the other's monogamous. Could be some internal story I haven't picked up yet. What if I check out their leisure hours?

James File

Cynthia File

Cottons Sports Club
London Bridge City
Tooley Street
London SE1

Members   4,474
Male   1,238
Female   3,236

Monthly Subscription   £72.50

14 Qualified Fitness Instructors: Dance, Aerobics, Gym, Weights, Well Being,
Yoga

All new members must have a fitness assessment before using facilities.

Members List Search >>>

James Cameron member since Dec. 1997

Cynthia Shepherd member since June 1997

I run their names against lists at health clubs. Robert no show. James belongs to Cottons.

So does a Ms C. Shepherd.

James is five feet ten inches and over thirteen stone. He's overweight, not massively, but the tendency is there. He's a prime work-out boy. She's five feet six inches and eight stone. Thin.

Well, at least we know their fitness levels. On their original assessments, James and Cynthia were both intermediates. Pulse rate at rest below sixty-five.

Ah, but a gym membership tells you much more than the heart rate; it's where so many hearts beat too. Their memberships go back a while, two years. To the time when James was sharing with Robert, alone. Maybe not conclusive, but I'd guess the couple in this ménage is James and Cynthia.

James File

Cynthia File

Robert File

Vodafone	You Are Here
James Cameron	Mobile: 0777 242 1649
Cynthia Shepherd	Mobile: 07694 297 614
Robert Bolton	Mobile: 07962 783 411

Call Match: last 50 calls

07694 297 614 to 0777 242 1649
12 calls   8 a.m.–1 p.m.: 6; 1 p.m.–6 p.m.: 4;
                        6 p.m.–12 a.m.: 2

07694 297 614 to 07962 783 411
None

0777 242 1649 to 07694 297 614
18 calls   8a.m.–1 p.m.: 4; 1 p.m.–6 p.m.: 12;
                        6 p.m.–12 a.m.: 2

Follow up the hunch. Check up on their mobile phone accounts. James calls Cynthia once or twice a day, especially towards evening ['Sorry I'm going to be a bit late, darling']. Cynthia never calls Robert; Cynthia only calls James.

Not conclusive, but the picture's emerging. Two lovers: James and Cynthia. Robert: the best mate. Wonder how all three get on, sharing like that? Does Cynthia like Robert? Is Robert in the middle? How difficult life can get, when you play the couples game.

James File

www.TheKnot.com

MARRIAGE & DIVORCE
RECORDS SPECIALISTS

Searching . . .

James Cameron – Sophie Cameron [Eldridge]
Decree Absolute   12/01/94
Marriage   2 years
Grounds   Adultery
Cited   Keith Featherstone

Settlement figures . . . please wait . . .

Searching please wait . . .

Sophie Eldridge >>>

Marriage >>>

Guildford Register Office   15/05/94

Keith Arnold Featherstone – Sophie Christina Eldridge [both previously divorced]

UK Criminal Records

CASE 3434/5THT/93
Sophie Christina Cameron: illegal breaking and entering Isis Research Laboratories, Oxon, 13/11/93.

The couples game. Got me going. Friends, partners, marriage . . . divorce. An interesting lead. James was married before. Could be that Mr C isn't a Mr – maybe he's a she. The ex-wife checking up on who young James is getting hitched to this time round.

The ex-Mrs Cameron was originally Miss Eldridge. Sophie Christina Eldridge, no less. She's nine years older than James. They had a quick divorce. No children. Minimal settlement. Grounds for divorce: her adultery. The person cited: Keith Featherstone.

I check out Sophie. She is now Mrs Featherstone.

And what about this – she also has a criminal record. Broke into an animal-testing lab near Oxford and destroyed the research files. In '93. But that was when she was still married to James. James married to an Animal Rights activist? We need to know more about this little plum.

match Sophie Cameron>>>UKnews.local

OXFORD EVENING POST
19/08/93

Animal Rights Extremists Attack Isis Research Laboratory:
Two Charged. Mystery over Third Man

for full text >>>

The incident occurred at Isis Research. At night three masked raiders enter the laboratories and destroy computer files representing four years of research work into deficiencies in young children's eyesight – which also involved 'testing' the eyesight of perfectly healthy mice, rats and – wait for the killer blow – kittens. Oh my God! Outrage in anthropomorphic fallacy land! 'They're blinding kittens!' Calls for Direct Action.

So they break in, hack into the computers, destroy the files. No doubt messages were left daubed on the screens. *Don't Fuck with Nature* in red spray paint, one imagines, just for effect.

Only trouble is, two of the three raiders take off their masks in the car park. Caught on the security camera. Sophie and a certain Keith Featherstone. The third member of the gang is never identified. Well, he did have the presence of mind to keep his mask on until they'd left the premises.

Who was the third man?

I don't know. You don't know. But we can have a good old-fashioned guess.

James the activist? Doesn't add up to Dogg. But then we all do odd things when we're twenty-six and married to an older woman who eats muesli for breakfast and sends out nail bombs in the afternoon post.

Sophie hid James's identity back then, but maybe she now wants some kind of payback. Or she wants to warn the possible new Mrs James Cameron about something deep and dark in James's nature.

20/01/00   08.45

From: thedogg@acdogg.co.uk
To: samc@riverso.co.uk
Subject: Garden Flat, 81 Bryanston Road

Later, I write a long report to Mr Collier. A good breakdown of James and Cynthia and Robert. Nice detail. Who they are, what they buy, what sort of people we're dealing with. I write an especially eloquent entry about the attack on Isis Research. Even ask the question: Was James there that night?

I get the same old message back:

> Dogg
> Can't you do any better than that?
> Who are they?

Wrong play, Dogg. Mr C isn't interested in your little theory about James. Still, it could just be that Mr C has got hooked on the data. Wants to know more. Like I said, once private clients get a taste for the information I give them, they keep wanting more. And that's how I make a living.

SUPERCOOL LINKS

The Secret Surrealist Society [202.337.0022] :epacsteN

Virtual Gallery

DISiFoRmAtIOn

Scanner Links We believe in Scanning around Here !!!
artmuseum
activist
Bigbrother
DharmaRoad
DarksideGothic

AND remember God Loves You

www.surrealist.com

Welcome to Surrealist.com. This site is continuing to bring the world of
Surrealism to the masses.

Surrealism was a means of reuniting conscious and unconscious realms of
experience so completely that the world of dream and fantasy would be joined
to the everyday rational world in 'an absolute reality, a surreality'.

All three of my protégés are achievers; all three of them know how to fit in.

The Dogg has never known how to fit in. Except with things digital. Shall we say I wasn't a good mixer, as I still am not.

Outside it is dark. The streetlights are on. It feels like one of those evenings that René Magritte would paint. Like the Empire of Lights, when the sky is bright but the streetscape is dark. Hard to tell what is real. Specially if you're a bit surreal like René.

I think about René quite a lot. Visited an exhibition of his work in Barcelona last autumn, on the net: webcams, still images, full monty. Cool stuff. Love his attention to detail. The meticulous draughtsmanship in the hands of a man who could see there was no point in painting what he could see.

René had a way with him. 'I detest my past and anyone else's,' he said – well, he did come from Belgium so that's forgivable. 'I detest the decorative arts, folklore, advertising, voices making announcements, aerodynamism, boy scouts, the smell of mothballs, events of the moment, and drunken people.' Hey, René, whoa boy. But I know what you're getting at. I detest the past, yet I am always drawn back to it, because the past has data. Or data has a past which you can make present.

What I'm beginning to discover is that I can make the past into the now. Because facts are always in the now. Facts are always alive, the continuous present that never fades. That's why I can bring things to life, René. And that's what you were doing in paint. You went for the internal story extraordinaire. You and the Surrealists. The Surrealists tell us that there's only life internal; that the internal is the answer to everything. Life's an illusion.

Brave attempt at an explanation, René, but for the Dogg's money, that's just posturing – like Salvador Dali's moustache. You say there are no facts. I say there are only facts.

I think on the Empire of Lights. In between the dark and the light; considering my position.

THIS IS YOUR COMPUTER ON DRUGS

@@

/~

0

www.botspot.com

WHAT'S A BOT?

In short: A **bot** is a software tool for digging through data. You give a bot directions and it brings back answers.

The word is short for robot of course, which is derived from the Czech word robota meaning work.

On the Web, robots have taken on a new form of life. Since all Web servers are connected, robot-like software is the perfect way to perform the methodical searches needed to find information.

For example, Web search engines send out robots that **crawl** from one server to another, compiling the enormous lists of URLs that are at the heart of every search engine. Shopping bots compile enormous databases of products sold at on-line stores.

The term bot has become interchangeable with **agent**, to indicate that the software can be sent out on a mission, usually to find information and report back. Strictly speaking, an agent is a bot that goes out on a mission. Some bots operate in place; for example, a bot in Microsoft Front Page automates work on a Web page.

Bots have great potential in **data mining**, the process of finding patterns in enormous amounts of data. Because data mining often requires a series of searches, bots can save labour as they persist in a search, refining it as they go along. Intelligent bots can make decisions based on past experiences, which will become an important tool for data miners trying to perfect complex searches that delve into billions of data points.

I have a past.

I have sought the lost. I have found children from broken marriages, snatched by the desperate parent. I have revealed the illegitimate; I have undermined the legitimate. I have exposed the chief executive on the take. I have planted information on the wrong files. I have ruined reputations. I have shown that money destined for famine aid ends up in Swiss bank accounts. I have tracked down the dead to a new life in South Africa. I have identified the money launderer. I have opened the files on corrupt politicians. I have even worked for the press.

That was all in the job. I was just doing what I was told.

But somehow what I am into right now is different. Then I had limits, and clear objectives. With this contract there are no limits. I am just swimming in the data stream, floating in @, waiting to see what Mr C really wants.

And here in @, there are no rules. You make them up. Some people don't like this much. They think they own their information. But they don't. It's a free bird that's flown.

You don't own them, but you exist as facts out there in cyberspace – even misleading or erroneous facts. Often you will not know or realize that you have left data trails; more alarmingly you may not even be aware of the facts themselves. Somebody else writes something about you, it gets stored on some database, and suddenly it's a fact. It's become part of the you that rests out there, part of your identity. That's why I always look for patterns, not individual bits of data. If something doesn't fit the pattern, I can check it out.

IMPROVE THE SECURITY OF YOUR SITE BY BREAKING INTO IT

BY DAN FARMER

A deadly creature that can both strike poisonously and hide its tracks without a whisper or a hint of a trail. The Uebercracker is here . . .

TECHNIQUES ADOPTED BY 'SYSTEM CRACKERS' WHEN ATTEMPTING TO BREAK INTO CORPORATE OR SENSITIVE PRIVATE NETWORKS

A very small percentage of crackers actually define targets and attempt to attack them. Such crackers are far more skilled and adopt 'cutting edge' techniques to compromise networks . . . Such crackers are also known to have access to exploits and tools used by security consultants and large security companies, and then to use them to scan defined targets for all known remote vulnerabilities.

A typical corporation will have an Internet presence for the following purposes:
The hosting of corporate webservers
E-mail and other global communications via the Internet
To give employees access to the Internet

In such environments, the corporate webservers and mailservers are usually kept 'outside' the corporate network and then information is passed via trusted channels onto the corporate network.

In the case of trust present between external mailservers and hosts on the corporate network, a well-thought filtering policy has to be put in effect . . . From a security standpoint such hosts that operate on multiple networks can pose a massive threat to network security, as upon compromising a host, it then acts as a simple 'bridge' between networks.

Front-Line Information Security Team (FIST)

The Dogg is a detective. Some would say I'm some common hacker with a fantasy. Wrong. The Dogg has the juice. Making the big connection to the starry halo which is life.

To survive as a data detective you have to stay anonymous *and* you have to stay out of jail. Getting caught does serious damage to your income potential. Keeping out of jail means sticking to the rules. First Rule: computers talk to computers. Most hackers make the mistake of staying human: man against the machine. Cracking, to them, is a game, it's all about the wit of man outwitting the machine. This explains why hackers and crackers take so long to break into a system and why most of them get caught. Cracking is not about man against machine [the man always leaves tracks], it's about *becoming* the machine. Entering the source code; mimicking the genes. If a computer thinks that you're another computer – especially another friendly computer that they've been programmed to communicate with – then they'll blab about anything you want them to. They literally can't stop talking. It's not in their nature, poor loves. No truth serum required. They just splurge the lot. To get the info you have to get to be another computer.

Second Rule: computers talk to computers. What does that mean, dummy? Computers are born to communicate and they hate being alone. They like it best in networks. They're happiest when they're all hooked up. Now, this is their weakness. They trust one another. In fact, they're programmed to, otherwise they couldn't communicate. Study a network – any network, even the Internet – and you'll soon find some of the systems are designated as 'trusted hosts'. These are host computers connected into the network, and used as trusted elements or sources from which information can be exchanged. The way to get to the system you're after is to become a trusted host. One of the Dogg's favourite methods is to plant a 'sniffer' program inside a network which will establish the hosts and tell you who's trusted. The trusted hosts are easier to crack – it's their job to communicate. And that's where I get in. From then on it's like pillow talk: all the others cosy up around you and whisper sweet nothings.

Maybe you don't need to know any of this. But it might make you think differently about my art.

www.prs.net/schubert.html

CLASSICAL MIDI ARCHIVES – SCHUBERT

The Classical Midi Archives contain thousands of classical music files you can listen to at the click of your mouse. Most composers are represented.

www.smusic.com/paxos/schubert

SCHUBERT, FRANZ [1797–1828]

Schubert, Franz. The son of a schoolmaster who had settled in Vienna . . .

www.phllclass.polygram

FRANZ SCHUBERT

Franz Schubert [bio] HOME 2 Marches Charactéristiques, D886, – 3 Klavierstucker . . .

w3.rz-berlin.mpg.de/cmp/schubert

FRANZ SCHUBERT

Epoch:Country:Austria [1797–1828] Detailed information about: Songs. Symphonies. Chamber Music. Piano Music. Sacred Music. Opera . . .

Dogg keeps on shifting. I don't have an office with 'Private Detective' on the glass door. I don't have a secretary to take calls and flirt with. I carry everything I need. Having a base inevitably builds up the stuff you have to deal with: if you want to achieve the paperless office, don't have an office.

There are many other professions in the electronic domain which are mobile, but none as 'anywhere, anytime, for anyone' as the data sleuth. My clients could be in LA or Berlin. I don't have to be anywhere specific to take on the job. I follow information. You could say I'm the beginning of the new generation of ultimate mobile workers – to which I'd reply, are there any other sort of workers?

In the evening, music. I listen to Schubert. String Quintet in C Major. The slow movement. It's pure yearning, or what the Germans neatly call *Sehnsucht*. It reminds me of John Keats. The Odes are full of long-ing. Like the Bold Lover on the Grecian Urn.

> Bold Lover, never, never canst thou kiss,
> Though winning near the goal – yet do not grieve . . .

What is longing? An intimation of the soul? Stretching for something which is always just out of reach.

I wonder whether James or Cynthia or Robert long for things. Then I remind myself not to get into that internal story stuff too much. I have to understand these people but that doesn't mean I should get involved with them. It's all too easy to get sucked in, suckered in. These people are prints on the trail.

A technique I learnt some time ago: if your mind's gone fuzzy and you can't see where the trail leads, just find out what your suspects had for dinner. It gets your mind back on the everyday detail, on the search for the elusive, explosive fact. And you are what you eat, after all.

Sainsbury's

MAKING LIFE TASTE BETTER

Tesco

EVERY LITTLE COUNTS

ASDA

THAT'S ASDA PRICE

Almost all consumer categories covered

The carefully constructed questionnaires give you detailed information for practically every consumer category imaginable. This is because we have designed them specifically to deal with almost every aspect of people's lives. Where they live, how they live, their habits, their aspirations and their attitudes: how they spend their money, how they save their money, and what they intend to buy – now and in the future.

Call our Data Rental Team NOW.

Here's a list of some of the products that James, Robert and Cynthia have bought today:

Boots egg mayo sandwich; Evian; Johnson's Cotton Buds; Budweiser six-pack; Birds Eye frozen peas; Dove soap; 12 Extra Safe Durex; Andrex toilet paper [cornflower blue]; Sainsbury's Caesar salad; *FHM*; *The Times*; Porkinson sausages; Penfold's Bin 61 Cabernet Sauvignon; The Doors CD; semi-skimmed milk; fresh basil; Tampax 32-pack tampons; 10 Marlboro Lights; *Financial Times*; *Country Life*; Sainsbury's Stone Bake Pizza; aluminium foil; Hovis brown loaf thick cut; Lurpak butter [slightly salted]; Brecon Hills water; slimline tonic water; Berocca Vitamin C; Sainsbury's muesli [de luxe]; 42 litres 4-star petrol [BP].

Seems such a normal, insignificant list, doesn't it? You could try guessing which characters bought what, but why waste your breath? The people that matter already know. Every item on this list is tagged back to a database somewhere. And if the marketing men could get hold of all this information at once, imagine what webs they could spin. That's what they're after, the complete picture, joining up the lines between the dots. Make the pattern. In this case they would see an affluent household [Andrex toilet tissue, Brecon Hills water], mixed [*FHM*, Tampax], into music and Italian food, and ambitious [*Country Life*].

Typical urban professionals.

29/01/00 04.50 status

James File

James Cameron

Bank accounts	Lloyds TSB Current a/c 331690 84216940	£9,7521.61
	Lloyds TSB Deposit a/c 331690 98744126	£52,950.12
	C & G Postal a/c T6426008219	£6,100.05
Credit Cards	Lloyds Mcard 4775 9180 2227 4176 Exp. 12/00 American Express 37176582147721 Exp. 09/00	
Mortgage	Garden Flat, 81 Bryanston Rd, NW6 8KR Purchased 1995 [original mortgage £100,000.00] C & G Interest Only £30,000.00	£171.00 p.m.
Savings	PEP: HSBC Index Tracker Fund	£25,098.00
	ISA: Invesco [American Fund]	£7,490.00
	M & G UTSP Japanese Smaller Co's	£11,450.00
	Barings Emerging Markets Unit Trusts	£18,756.00
	TESSA Britannia	£4,800.00
Shares held: UK	British Telecom	500
	BP	901
	Shell Transport and Trading	754
	Marks & Spencer	1500
	Prudential	680
	Lloyds TSB	2,400
Store Cards	Selfridges 3376 48 7452 9762 3148 Exp. 04/01	£98.00
	John Lewis 9761 89414	£168.25
	Marks & Spencer 1181 41 7641 823 5749 Exp. 09/01	£34.90
	Austin Reed 022C 117219	£00.00
Loyalty Card	BA Executive Club [Gold] No. 7388219	400 pts, 27,490 air miles

Now I've got three trails that run separately, cross and recross, and go to ground.

What am I tracking? It's the old logic: 'Follow the money.' Except, for the data sleuth, that becomes 'You are what you spend.' After bricks and mortar, the next best way to get your scent is the financials. In fact, what you spend, where you spend it and how often, will, in my experience, lead, well, yes, right on to the money.

James has a classic profile. Nothing remarkable at first glance, you'd think. Mr Continuity stamped all over the file. Banks with Lloyds TSB, run of the mill but a sensible choice; as an accountant he knows better than most. Has Good Savings. High Net Worth-ish.

The mortgage on 81 Bryanston Road is in his sole name and much of it has been paid off. Solid share portfolio: good spread, small exposure to emerging markets, no Biotech stock, nothing that spells unwarranted risk. Store cards at Selfridges and Austin Reed show a preference for upscale shopping – James is queuing up with a smarter professional crowd on the weekend. All conservative stuff. No hint of the activist.

James's mobile phone is paid for by the company. He's got a personal on-line account with a well-known provider. He's not a techie. So where does he get his kicks?

29/01/00 04.50 status

James File

James Cameron

Subscriptions	*Autocar*	[03/01]	
	Car Magazine	[03/01]	
	Rugby Monthly	[09/00]	
	Wine	[11/00]	
	Private Eye	[07/00]	
Standing Orders	British Telecom	£55.00	p.m.
	C & G	£171.00	p.m.
	Cottons Health Club	£72.50	p.m.
Direct Debits	Worldwide Fund for Nature	£50.00	p.a.
	Dian Fossey Gorilla Fund	£50.00	p.a.
TV/Cable Package	Sky Digital – Sky Sports World	£34.99	p.m.

Three car magazines a month. Healthy male interests give out a physical perspective on life. What's this? *Rugby Monthly*'s also on the list. Hard cars, contact sports, solid finances: James likes measurable things.

Direct debits: Sky Digital with a Sky sports package. Here's Mr Continuity again: boy's stuff, but no big spending.

James's softer side is also there on the money files. Two DDs to charities. A modern gospel: though I speak fluent French and summer in Tuscany, if I have not charity on my direct debits I am become as a sounding brass, or a tinkling cymbal. As I have experienced many times, the love of fluffy, feathered or scaled beasts who share this planet with us goes deep into the human psyche. Especially when you get to eighty-five. Fur is thicker than water when it comes to dividing up your estate. How else can you explain all those crones who leave zillions to cats' homes? Cats, I ask you! The Brighton and Worthing Home for Felines, for instance, has more money than most pension funds. Pretty soon I'm going to do some serious investigating into that place – I want to get a picture of the ravaged minds behind the donations. What sort of people are these? What drives them? What keeps them going for eight or nine decades, only to give it all away to cats? Not that I'm biased in these matters, of course.

Back to the scent. James makes two wildlife donations; the first generic, the second species specific. That's quite normal: you love football, but you support Arsenal. But not for James some sub-species. James goes for the big and obvious. Gorillas. Well, he was married to an Animal Rights activist, first time round.

Cynthia File

Cynthia Shepherd

Court date	20/04/93
Case number	6704811
Court name	Hackney
Action brought by	Ms Cynthia Jane Shepherd
Case status	Dismissed 20/04/93

Traffic Offences	2 speeding fines
	6 points

Before I went to the money files on Cynthia I had to clear up a suspicion. That donation to the Rape Crisis Centre. One little entry that had a whole stack of history behind it. A blip that blasts.

Next stop the Criminal Court Records. Oh, Dogg, sometimes your hunches should not be right. They are the stuff of bad dreams, and sometimes I worry that the bad dreams filter onto reality. They make things happen.

There it is. Name, number, case dismissed. The charge was rape. That takes big courage to pursue. She had to have been convinced. But Cynthia didn't win her case. [Interesting, if other people deny a fact, does that make it less real?] Not even with the advice of the Rape Crisis Centre – why else would she now be sending them donations? So Cynthia, well advised, full of anger and self-loathing, gets turned away. Why? She didn't have the facts to nail him with.

No, worse than that. In his defence, the accused says that Cynthia agreed to sex. Why? Because she was bound up.

Cynthia denied all this. Sure, they'd had sex before; and yes, she had been tied up. But she hadn't agreed on *this* occasion. You can just hear the lawyer seize on the comment, can't you?

'Oh, so you agreed on other occasions?'

'Yes – but only for a bit of fun. Nothing like this. And I didn't consent on this occasion . . .'

Poor Cynthia, in that instant you lost the case. Just because you told the truth.

Bad things happen, Cynthia. There is no return to innocence. The facts cannot be undone, even though others can't see them. Inside you can turn away, your inner life can say it did not happen. But it did. You know it did. You scream it did. But no-one is listening. Except me. Or maybe Mr C?

On average, an adult living in a metropolitan area gets filmed by 25 security cameras each day.

Plastic Card Payments

UK	1991	1994	1998
All cards [millions]	2,011	2,914	4,847
Value [£billions]	85	128	228

Source: Association of Payment Clearing Services

Is that what Mr C is after: the rape trial?

I send another e-mail. No long report. Just the details of the rape case from the records.

The next day I get the reply:

> Thank you. Please continue. Payment will be made.

But is he pleased with the information on the rape trial, or does he simply want me to keep on going?

Hesitation. I have done the usual detective work. Fulfilled my obligations to the client. Do I just keep going, not knowing what this is all about? It's not as though I have a contract with Mr C. But the thing is that I like where I'm going. I'm not just tracking someone down, I'm creating someone. Like images on a security camera: a person walking through the frame, oblivious of the lens. I'm pushing the technology to its limits; finding new levels, where the electronic world morphs with the physical world. The recording meets the live event.

I think about it some more. Cynthia doesn't strike me as someone who would try for a false conviction on a charge like rape. There has to be a connection I'm missing about Cynthia.

04/02/00 07.34 status

Cynthia File

Cynthia Shepherd

Bank Accounts	Co-operative Bank 581290 61420072	£4,251.06
Savings Accounts	Co-operative Bank 581290 82466439	£6,020.00
	Halifax Building Society 1456 8325 2030 21714	£7,094.58
Credit Card	Co-operative Bank VISA 4550 9698 1291 7461 Exp. 03/01	£1,424.06
Store Cards	Marks & Spencer 11841 6653 8941 3841 Exp. 03/01	£112.40
	John Lewis 9761 37417	£24.00
	Russell & Bromley 9491 69141 3895 5811	£86.00
	Habitat 1120 13081 6341 6917	£0.00
	Liberty 9851 1483 1761 13341 Exp. 09/00	£216.00
Loyalty Cards	Boots [492148986]	980 pts
	Virgin Airline Freeway Club [Silver]	34 pts, 20,400 air miles
	British Airways [Blue]*	180 pts, 3,200 air miles
Subscriptions	*Marie Claire*	[08/00]
	Vogue	[08/00]
	Emmanuelle	[10/00]
	Sibyl	[11/00]
Charities [monthly]	Women Against Violence	£15.00
	Greenpeace	£10.00
	Friends of the Earth	£10.00
	National Abortion Campaign	£15.00

* Meal preference: Vegetarian

The financial info on Cynthia is all ups and downs, a sine wave. Some of the entries are right in line with what you'd expect from an anthropology graduate with a conscience. She has a current account with the Co-operative Bank. The Co-operative has made a name for taking a stance on ethical issues, the first to get into eco banking. Cynthia's bought into it, though of course she'd deny she was influenced by anything as obvious as positioning.

Her charity donations are on the button too. They're all issue-based, charities that champion a cause. Cynthia doesn't just want to save the whales, she wants to change the world.

But then the sine wave kicks in. She likes her home comforts. Wears her heart on silk sleeves. Take a look at her store cards. All good quality retailers. No tie-dyed T-shirts here. The tickets point to practical chic, prêt-à-porter Madonna. In the last month she has bought one trouser suit, two skirts and copious underwear. Well, not that copious in terms of size: she's a ten.

Then there are the subscriptions to *Vogue* and *Marie Claire*, the sort of high-fashion mags that you'd think would be out of the coffee-table reach of a conscience girl like Cynthia. Does she love expensive clothes, or is she after some feel-good factor, some comfort from beauty? I can relate to that, Cynthia. Everything's right in the *Vogue* world, girl. Beauty is truth here, and truth beauty.

And when she's not travelling in the realms of *Vogue*, Cynthia flies with Virgin. Her Virgin Airline Freeway shows she travels a lot. Getting away is good.

Ah, Cynthia, my Prada activist, why did you choose James?

<u>Trivia</u>
James – Gemini
Robert – Libra
Cynthia – Aries

<u>www.LifeGuide.co.uk</u>

LIFEGUIDE PRESENTS . . .

LOVEGUIDE

It has long been recognized by astrologers that well-suited and happy couples have compatibility mirrored in their natal charts – in far more depth and many more ways than that suggested merely by harmonizing Sun signs. The natal charts of well-matched couples frequently show favourable aspects between, for example, their Moon, Venus and Mars signs, in addition to an affinity between their Sun signs.

A loveguide for singles, this astrological world-wide dating service enables truly compatible people to find each other.

Let's imagine for a moment, play the storyteller. Perhaps James told Cynthia about his little scrape at the Isis Research Labs. She finds it attractive. Professional man with a conscience – a bit like her. Only does she talk about her past? No way of knowing. Maybe two vulnerable people getting together. Maybe two gym acquaintances who fancy each other. Mr C hasn't asked me to find out 'Why are they?', but 'Who are they?' For now, all we have is two people together. Are they in love? Can you ever tell? People say about others: 'They're very much in love.' But often that's a passing look, a passion that fades like a photograph left in sunlight.

True love doesn't look like love. It's harder, more restrained. Indifferently tender. Yet it will do anything, contemplate anything, achieve and destroy all things. The Dogg knows this to be true.

[In sickness and in health.] He has seen sacrifice. He has seen happiness. He has seen broken hearts. [Till death us do part.] He has seen murder. He has seen joy. All in the name of love.

The Dogg cannot explain this. Love is a fact which is only true for as long as it's true. There is love. People do love one another. But not always for ever.

How do you fall in love? Is it all fate? Two individuals who are meant to be with each other? If so, how can the heart recover from love lost? You will give up your life, gladly, to be with someone. And then a letter comes in the post: *I have met someone else, it's all over.* So now you can't fulfil that promise to yourself. You can't be what you want to be. The facts tell you that you are not with them, they're not with you. There's nothing you can do about it.

The Dogg says to all this: can't you show me nothing but surrender? Get up. Never give up.

04/02/00 06.30 status

Robert File

Robert Bolton

Bank Account	First Direct	£684.40
	791290 68335710	

Notes
Collections call 1 10/11/99
Collections call 2 14/12/99
Collections letter 2 16/12/99

	Max. balance:	£9,1720.06
	Min. balance:	− £3,2570.88
	No. of days overdrawn:	17

High Interest Savings Account	First Direct	£114.62
	791290 72811637	

Savings Account	Chelsea Building Society	£26.70
	[no transactions since 01/98]	

Credit Cards	Mastercard Gold Card	£2,410.69
	4323 7004 6110 9754 Exp. 09/00	
	Barclays VISA Card	£4,100.21
	4929 8112 7430 6139 Exp. 04/01	
	American Express [Corporate]	£3,510.00
	3714 982416 3428 Exp. 02/01	

Store Cards	Selfridges	£871.20
	3376 89745 8732 7642 Exp. 03/02	

Loyalty Cards	BA Executive Club [Silver] No. 7496821	130 pts
		13,110 air miles

Subscriptions	*New Statesman*	[04/00]
	Rallying	[07/00]
	New Yorker	[11/01]

Direct Debits	Labour Party	£50.00
	Shelter	£150.00

Where do you fit in with all this, Robert? Me, I'm a loner. A lone Dogg. I travel alone. You are alone, but maybe not a loner by choice. Advertising man. Modern male. How do you sleep these duvet nights?

To the uninitiated eye, it might seem like Robert's got life sorted. He banks with First Direct, the twenty-four-hour telephone bank launched in the early '90s. He was a classic early adopter, as they say in the trade; he signed up with First Direct a month after it started. To me that suggests he's decisive and accepts change readily. He also has a savings account with Chelsea Building Society. The branch is near his office in Charlotte Street. Convenience was probably the main item on the score card there. [Balance has been £26.70 for two years.]

But Robert's a spender, not a saver. He has four credit cards, which is at the high end of things in the UK. The list shows some status seeking: he bothered to get a Gold Card from NatWest. Gold Cards always smack of 'money maketh the man', that the victim's self-identity is linked to financial success. He's also managed to convince his employers that he's worth two corporate cards.

He took out his supermarket store card with Sainsbury's after Cynthia moved in. A gesture of independence in the face of a crowding fridge. Well, it beats writing 'This belongs to Robert' on the butter. The rules of the house had changed and he wasn't going to let it go unnoticed.

On the DD side there's a couple of interesting signals; and they both point Left. He makes a donation to the Labour Party and subscribes to the *New Statesman*. Robert is a socialist. Now, Dogg has no bone to pick with such sympathies. Dogg is not a political animal. Dogg is not interested in your politics *per se*. I'm interested in where they fit, or don't fit, into the pattern. In your case, Robert, it takes me right back to your childhood. Your dad was a teacher of sorts – pinko probably. So the socialism is deep-seated, it goes beyond a fad or temporary disaffection with the other side.

It seems to me that this sort of background would make you fairly careful about money, Robert. But not a bit of it. Credit cards, early adopter, you could be a bit of a dodger. A chancer even. You were kicked out of school, remember?

04/02/00 06.40 status

Robert File

Robert Bolton

Credit File Experian Ref. 39124779C
Mr R. Bolton, 81 Bryanston Road, London NW6 8KR

MASTERCARD GOLD CARD
Started 10/07/98
Balance £4,802.51
Status history 000123401200
In past 36 months, no. of status 1–2 is 4, no. of status 3+ is 2

BARCLAYS VISA CREDIT CARD/REVOLVING CRE
Started 04/02/94
Balance £3,110.08
Status history 001234001230
In past 36 months, no. of status 1–2 is 4, no. of status 3+ is 3

Details updated 10/12/99

Status Code	Meaning
0	payment up to date
1	payment up to one month late
2	payment up to two months late
3	payment up to three months late
4	payment up to four months late
U	account status unclassified
D	account dormant or inactive
8/9	account defaulted

A credit check will tell you a lot about a person's weaknesses. This is where the cracks first appear. Partly because the credit companies are so good at what they do – they're in the data, not the money, business. And partly because most people turn to credit to run their lives. It's so easy. Just put it on the card, get up and walk away. You can calculate the APR, but what are you paying in privacy? Most people never stop to think that every purchase is being watched and recorded. And don't think on-line purchasing is any different – every time you click the buy button, you're telling people like me all about your secret likes, just as surely as if you'd sent me an e-mail:

> > Dear Dogg, I thought you'd like to know I buy sex toys on the Internet. I'm not proud of this, but my wife's gotta have them. It started out, as these things do, for a lark. Just a pair of handcuffs. Now it's strap-ons, remote control vibrators, Tantric massage creams ... where will it stop? I'm obsessed with on-line toy shopping. Yours, Curtis.

Every purchase is a confession.

The on-line world is ruthless: all will be revealed. Every little fault will be known, not to dictator governments or secret-service agencies. Forget that Big Brother conspiracy – though it's there all right. Big Brother is not the real enemy. The real enemy is you and me. We're the ones that want to know. Everyman is the threat. We have to decide just how far we want to push it.

In Robert's case I'd guess there's much to discover down the search line. But the first information is clear. Robert has got money problems. That makes me twitch: something here that doesn't compute. Good job, no mortgage, and shares a house so he can't be paying a huge rent. Yet Robert's always behind on the credit-card payments. Lots of late payments and really big sums outstanding. He's borrowing at way over the odds: to finance a lifestyle or to pay for a weakness? Both are dangerous because both get you noticed.

Often it's not what you spend, but how you spend it that's the key. Small amounts frequently, less of a problem. But big sums at a time and we're talking trouble.

04/02/00 05.34 status

<u>Robert File</u>

Robert Bolton

Bank Account	First Direct 791290 68335710	
Credit zone	£5,000.00	

<u>Date</u>	<u>Item</u>	<u>Amount</u>
04/01	Cash	£400.00
07/01	Cash	£350.00
10/01	Cash	£400.00
13/01	Cash	£150.00
18/01	Cash	£400.00
24/01	Cash	£300.00
28/01	Cash	£400.00
Credit Card	Mastercard Gold Card 4323 7004 6110 9754 Exp. 09/00	
15/01	Armani [Knightsbridge]	£615.00
15/01	Titanic [Restaurant]	£128.00
	Met Bar	£48.00
12/01	Momo's [Restaurant]	£148.00

So far as lifestyle goes Robert certainly has a hand in the cookie jar. He wears Polo casual shirts and smart ones from Thomas Pink. Church's shoes. He buys suits from Armani. [By the way, the sales code shows he's a 42 long.] He goes there at least once a month. That's regular shopping in my book. [How would you look in an Armani, Dogg? More cool, probably. As you take your daily walk beside the Pacific Ocean, will the wolf whistles rifle through the clear blue air? Is LA ready for you?]

The odd restaurant bill doesn't tell much at this stage. £140 or so for two shows it was a smart restaurant; maybe he was trying to impress someone.

But it's the cash withdrawals that are the business. Robert takes out £400 every three or four days. Now, at first glance, you might think that cash is a problem for me. Well, yes and no. Sure, I can't know what he's spending it on. But then again, I know he's taking out cash, so he's probably spending it on a particular type of purchase. And he's spending in a particular type of world. That's the kind of information I get hot on.

Now let's deduce for a moment. What do you spend a few hundred pounds on every two or three days – in a cash world? Gambling, sex, drugs, paying off debts? It's got to be somewhere in that arena.

A quick track through the phone bill. No regular calls to his bookmaker. And admit it, as an advertising man he isn't that likely to nip off for the afternoon down to his local bookie. If he was spending on the horses he'd be tele-betting.

So I think that leaves us with sex or drugs. If I were to open a window on his private medical records what do you think that I'd find?

04/02/00 06.57

<u>Robert File</u>

MediSearch . . . accessing files Dr William Arbuthnot . . .
patient: Robert Bolton
12/11/99

C/O poor sleep, lack of energy. Appetite poor, weight loss. No allergies. 55 units alcohol per wk [brandy]. Long chat. Admits to being long-term drug abuser. Snorts cocaine, injects heroin.

Diagnosis: Alcoholic depressant, drug abuse. Suggest referral to DDU for assessment. Gave him numbers for. Follow up one month.

Medical records are held on files just like everything else. Only thing is they're entered optically as original notes, so you have to have some voiceware to read out. But that's not too tough. And they make good listening, great books at bedtime.

It's simple. Robert spends the cash on drugs. Those are the bare facts. Suppose this was the first thing we'd uncovered about Robert – what would we have made of that? Or if we met him casually and knew all of this on first acquaintance? How would we treat him differently? Edged away, even though he was intelligent and charming?

And what picture would we build of someone if we just had their medical records to go on? Say the girl you met in the bar last night, or the guy at that friend's party. Because, after all, medical records are some of the most intimate facts you can get on a person. Way beyond the CV when it comes to insights. What a world it would be: can you wait?

Personally the Dogg is ambivalent towards medical notes. These are facts. Absolutely. But they're a bit fuzzy nonetheless. You can see opinion and judgement creeping in here. Notice, for example, the word 'abuse' not 'use' in the notes. Tells us as much about the doctor as it does about the patient.

The doctor takes a look at you and makes a set of assumptions based on his experience and skill. They may be right. But some of the edges to these observations might be a little frayed. No matter though. They go down on your file. And then they're facts. Of course, if you have ever been wrongly diagnosed, you may not feel all that comfortable about this.

Cocaine

BY BYRON ALDSWORTH

Cocaine's physical effects may be less easily identified, but can be equally severe, especially for those who opt to snort the drug. Damage to blood vessels may lead to holes in the supporting tissue of the nose, indeed some damage will be done on the very first time the drug is snorted.

All that aside, Robert's file is unambiguous. And I'd say Robert's been doing drugs for some time. Since school or university, so James is bound to know about it – in fact they even share the same doctor. Now Robert's got more cash. More temptation. Easy access. And a whole lot of reasons he can give himself to justify the habit. It's only every now and then. It's the pressure of work. No. Can't be. I see Robert getting off on the pressure. Advertising company, lots of cool people, impossible deadlines – yet somehow he meets them. The next job. The next pitch. The next win.

But even this is not enough. Robert wants to feel different to everyone else, not just human but superhuman. That's the advertising line: 'Cocaine. It makes a good man great.'

But the explanations aren't reliable data. The Dogg feels for the excuses, but cannot accept them as data. Take the facts at face value, that's the way to reality. Robert has a habit. He has a weakness. Facing up to life is too hard to do all the time. Robert can handle it for the most part, but he also has to get away. He has to see things in a land of grey and pink. It's simple escapism. Trouble is, the more you escape, the more you want to get away.

Cynthia travels a lot; she likes to get away too. Got quite a bit in common with Robert; far more than with James, you could argue. Maybe Cynthia and Robert share the reverie of broken dreams. The knowledge of good and evil, that's what drove us out of the garden way back when and still drives us now. Knowledge.

THE TEMPEST SUMMARY AKA CLIFF NOTES

A SUMMARY OF THE TALE BY WILLIAM SHAKESPEARE

The Tempest
by William Shakespeare [1564–1616]

Type of Work:
Romantic fantasy

Setting:
A remote island; fifteenth century

Principal Characters:
Prospero, the rightful Duke of Milan, cast away on an island in the sea
Miranda, his beautiful daughter
Alonso, King of Naples
Ferdinand, Alonso's son
Antonio, Prospero's wicked brother, and false Duke of Milan
Sebastian, Alonso's brother
Gonzalo, a kind philosopher
Trinculo and Stephano, two drunken courtiers
Ariel, Prospero's spirit servant
Caliban, Prospero's grotesque slave monster

'. . . the other creature, Caliban, son of Sycorax, was a lumbering, deformed, half-savage figure.'

The World's Largest Literary Café: www.starbuck.com/shakespeare/The Tempesthall

Samuel Johnson said: 'Knowledge is of two kinds. We know a subject ourselves, or we know where we can find information upon it.'

Or you could put it another way. There aren't just two types of knowledge, but two types of people: those who know stuff and those who can find stuff out. Those who know stuff are superior, the brainy ones. Those who can find stuff out are paid by those who know things to find out more stuff so that they can know even more things.

But now everything is knowable, findable, quarry to the search engine. This is the Big Switch. The Dogg says that it shifts the balance. There's no need to know things any more, to carry them around in your head. Now you can find out everything, anytime. On a WAP phone. What's the point in education when everything is knowable? Bet the legislators haven't thought of that.

And with all this comes a new order. Now it's the searcher, not the magus, who has the upper hand. ''Ban. 'Ban Ca-Caliban. Has a new master. Get a new man.' Throw away Prospero's books – you can get it all on-line.

The hackers understand this. Hackers are doing what we all do, but taking it further. Taking it to its logical conclusion. Knowledge is open. So you can't cordon off neat little acres and say, 'No walking on the grass'. It's an open field. Begs the question: Why are hackers vilified, criminalized? Answer: Because we all have secrets. And we're deep down terrified our secrets will be known.

Secrets are part of people. A little essence of ourselves that we need to own, essential to our sense of identity. We have to feel we know more about ourselves than other people. That way we can be in control of ourselves: 'I'm the best judge of who the real me is. And that there secret just isn't part of the real-me picture. It's all a terrible mistake. Not me at all.'

But the secret is part of you. Cynthia was raped. James has hacked. Robert takes drugs.

How about the rest of us? Do we really want our lives to be laid open? It's up to you. Do you want to know? How much do you want to know?

09/02/00 12.41

From: thedogg@acdogg.co.uk
To: samc@riverso.co.uk
Subject: Garden Flat, 81 Bryanston Road

Me, I'm here at this screen and I think of innocence. The state of no knowledge, no connections. Is that truly happiness?

And as I'm searching, I wonder whether what protects us isn't knowing, but trusting. You don't want to know about your neighbour, because you want to trust them so that they'll trust you. Good societies are built on trust. Not knowing more, but trusting more. Trust is the great protector.

Trouble is, you have to be strong to trust. Not everyone's strong.

I'm just musing on all this, putting together a simple resumé of the Mr C case:

Unknown client, Sam Collier, sends me mail out of the blue. Tells me to check out an address. Electoral roll throws up James and Robert. Also discover that there's a third person, Cynthia, living at the same address. I send off the basics. Not good enough. He wants to know: Who are they?

I dig some more. Find out who they are, what they do: accountant, professional researcher, advertising exec. I find stuff about their background: where they went to university, who sleeps with whom and how they met [James and Robert at university; James and Cynthia probably met at the gym].

I go even further. Pluck out that Cynthia has been the victim of a rape. Brought it to trial but was unsuccessful. James has been married before. Briefly. 'No kids. No conviction.' Even though he was involved in a raid on a research lab in Oxfordshire. The other two – his former wife and her now husband – got nabbed. James got off. Robert is a chancer. Earns well, spends loads. The cash is going on 'charlie'.

I send the gist of this off to Mr C. I conclude:

> All three have secrets. Do you want me to press on these?

I get an e-mail straight back. Quick, almost too quick.

> Dogg
> I want to understand Robert.
> Go deeper.
> Sam Collier

I have seen the best minds of my generation destroyed by money. I have seen them dragging themselves through the angry streets looking for the next buck. I have seen cities which should be contemplating jazz do nothing but take the subway to work. People misled, confused, confounded. Feels like I'm heading into the badlands too. Becoming a bounty hunter.

Robert File

Pickfords Removals
'The Careful Movers'
www.pickfords.co.uk
16/02/00

Client	Robert Bolton
Address	81 Bryanston Road
	London NW6 8KR
Arrival Time	10.00
New Address	27 Cranleigh Gardens
	London SW6 5TT
Total	£450.00
Paid	VISA
Mr R. Bolton	4929 8112 7430 6139 Exp. 04/01

James File

jamesc@aandersen.co.uk
16/02/00

Log on	09.28
Total time logged	48 mins

Cynthia File

The Regency Hotel
Leamington Spa
16/02/00

1 Single Room	£120.00
Paid	VISA
Ms C. Shepherd	4550 9698 1291 7461 Exp. 03/01

Thames Trains [Timeways Travel]
16/02/00

Business First	£129.00		
Leamington Spa	Return		
Passenger	Ms C. Shepherd		
Seat Reservation	16/02/00	03B	08.26
	17/02/00	06B	18.34

Get this. Robert has moved out. To Fulham.

As anyone who lives in London will tell you, once you're a North Londoner you're always a North Londoner. So the move to family Fulham is a big change for Robert. Completely new environment, new walk to the tube in the morning, new late-night shop to get to know, new neighbours to politely ignore.

Robert's still renting. You might expect someone on his salary to have bought a place by now. The money he's spending on drugs is beginning to do damage. The nightmare is up and running.

He moved out on a Wednesday. Midweek, so he would have had to take a day off work. Even more telling is that the others wouldn't have been around to help him or to wave him off. [James logged onto his computer at work at nine thirty that day and Cynthia had bought train tickets to Leamington Spa and had booked into a hotel overnight.]

There was no team effort. No fond farewells. Rather sad; first there were two, then three, then three's a crowd.

16/02/00

Robert File

Tel. No. 020 7635 0579
27 Cranleigh Gardens
London SW6 5TT

Time	Number	Duration
18.20	020 7604 3490	1.40 mins
18.50	0161 941 5627	38.49 mins

Tel. No. 020 7604 3490
81 Bryanston Road
London NW6 8KR

Time	Number	Duration
18.25	020 7635 0579	2.26 mins

Two phone calls.

Remember Cynthia was away the night of Robert's move, staying at a hotel in Leamington Spa. Well, Robert calls James that evening. Couldn't have been much of a chat since they were only on the phone for one minute forty seconds. But that's not unusual between really close friends, is it? You develop this shorthand, or is it 'shortspeak'. Blokes don't do chatting much anyway; just make arrangements. So the conversation was short: Robert probably just telling James the move went OK and giving him his new number. Doggo, however, already has this number: all number changes are recorded so no big trick here, just scroll through the list until you find what you're looking for. Professional nous really.

A few minutes later, James calls Robert back. Again a short conversation.

Then Robert phones his mother. I don't see old Robert as a mummy's boy. From the records it looks as though he calls his mother maybe no more than twice a year. Short calls too. But this one, it's a major chat. Well, it's good to talk, isn't it? Just moved into a new home and feeling lonely; that's what mothers are for.

Probably nothing in it. But respect the rule: look for the pieces that don't fit the picture.

Robert File   file loading . . .

Cynthia File   file loading . . .

James File

jamesc@aandersen.co.uk
Lotus Notes

Diary
w/c 14/02/00
17/02 19.30   Robbo @ Che Bar
18/02   Leave for course
19/02   Reiki Course
20/02

A quick scan of James, Cynthia and Robert's diaries.

Robert and James plan to meet on Thursday. They're real friends. Very close. Want to keep the connection. When two guys have known each other for a time and then live together, an intimate relationship, a love develops. That doesn't move with a change of address.

Cynthia is going to a business event that night. James is away the following weekend at Reiki. Some conference, no doubt.

James File

jamesc@aandersen.co.uk
Lotus Notes

Diary
w/c 14/02/00
17/02 19.30   Robbo @ Che Bar [deleted]
18/02   Leave for course
19/02   Reiki Course
20/02

Mobile Tel. No. 0777 242 1649

Date	Time	Number	Duration
18/02	17.35	07962 783 411	4.26 mins

Robert and James don't meet.

James cancels. Work pressure, no doubt.

Nothing unusual in that. Don't get spooked by every little item. Keep a sense of proportion. You've got to decide which facts tell you something and which are dry.

Sure, I select which facts to emphasize. I select which to leave out. But everyone's involved in their own selection process. Creating their identity through the facts they choose to release. You do it all the time. It's how you cope with the problem of the two stories: the internal and the external. When you're introduced to someone, the conversation probably goes on to where they live and what they do. Two key factors in the identity game. After that, the choice of what information to release opens up – and we are all supremely adept at choosing what facts should become known to a perfect stranger.

This system of self-selection is changing, though. Imagine you're going for an interview. Time was when a few lines on a CV were all the facts they had to go on. You chose the facts, you made up the person you wanted to be. But now the interviewer can have every fact about you, from genetics to credit. They can choose what they believe is relevant; they can make you up. Life is selection; identity is selection. You are the facts. The big question is who's doing the choosing and when.

As a detective, I sort out the relevant from the random. If you had access to the same data as I do, would you make the same choices? No. You'd probably find a different story and discover different characters. You'd find different people. That's the spice of it.

Robert File

e-mail log robbo@saatchi-saatchi.com

Frequent Users

Week 46
alanh   8
janel   4
amandak   6
anitaj   15

Week 47
alanh   3
janel   .7
amandak   7
anitaj   17

anitaj   Jettison, Anita

Open staff file as anitaj@saatchi-saatchi.com. effective 04/02/00

Keep your objectivity. Another reason why I don't resort to reading people's e-mails. That sort of conversation is too personal. You think you know what's going on because you're reading words that people send to one another in private and therefore don't expect you to read. But just because something is written in private doesn't make it any more true. Too often people don't mean what they say, or say what they mean. That's why e-mail can send the detective in the wrong direction. The amateur will get all hot and bothered about some inappropriate remark and go scurrying off on a false chase. The Dogg's view: Better not to read them at all.

However, that's not to say that e-mail records are of no interest. Not at all. The Dogg can sense patterns from frequency. Robert gets regular e-mail from a couple of people at work. The frequency goes up and down, I'd guess, according to the status of the job they're all working on. The senders are alanh (copywriter), janel (accounts) and amandak (media). But the one that sticks out is anitaj. She's a production assistant. She sends him three e-mails a day. Every day.

anitaj is new to the e-mail list. Just joined the agency. New talent doesn't take long to get noticed – in advertising.

Robert File

Metro Cabs
Saatchi & Saatchi Account No 134

Date	Account	Name	Destination	Time
14/03	612	Robert Bolton	24b Waltham Street, SW3	7.57 p.m.
15/03	612	Robert Bolton	Saatchi & Saatchi	8.30 a.m.
			[pick-up 24b Waltham Street, SW3]	

UK REGISTER OF ELECTORS

Address:
24b Waltham Street
London SW3 7TH

1999
Anita Jettison

Robert moves out of the house in Bryanston Road. His best mate's shacked up with someone new. Robert starts getting regular e-mails from a woman at work. Nothing unusual in that. So where's the pattern?

Back to his phone account. I reckon he's out at least three times a week. No phone calls made on these nights, while on the others he makes at least three calls.

Would like to know where he's going. A slim chance, but I check out who Saatchi's use for cab bookings: Metro Cabs. Like all these cab companies, Metro Cabs have to keep a record of every fare. With a code for each user. Stops the secretaries from booking cabs for themselves – not that it always works, of course.

Et voilà, Dogg. Robert is taking cabs to an address in SW3 in the evening and back to the office in the morning. Match the address against the electoral register. The official residence of Ms Anita.

Robert File

Metro Cabs
Saatchi & Saatchi Account No. 134

Date	Account	Name	Destination	Time
16/03	612	Robert Bolton	24b Waltham Street, SW3	8.57 p.m.
17/03	612	Robert Bolton	Saatchi & Saatchi [pick-up 24b Waltham Street, SW3]	8.30 a.m.
20/03	612	Robert Bolton	Saatchi & Saatchi [pick-up 24b Waltham Street, SW3]	8.30 a.m.
22/03	612	Robert Bolton	Saatchi & Saatchi [pick-up 24b Waltham Street, SW3]	8.30 a.m.
23/03	612	Robert Bolton	81 Bryanston Road, NW6	8.30 p.m.

Robert is seeing Anita two or three times a week. Getting pretty serious. Want more? Robert's stopped withdrawing £400 in cash every few days. Could mean he's broken the habit, or that he's got closer to a supplier.

Another thing that worries me: Robert always goes to her place. Sure, he probably doesn't want the rest of the company to know about their liaison, so they avoid meeting in public. Still, why not back at his place? After all, the two of them are bound to be getting dovey by this stage.

Then something I hadn't noticed before. One of Cynthia's speeding fines. She got nabbed right close to home. One night before Robert moved out. Maybe, just maybe, she was driving away from home. Check Robert's cab account for that night. He went back to Bryanston Road at 8.45. Could be he was at home when Cynthia left.

One other thing, Robert doesn't call Anita at home on the nights that they're not together. And she doesn't call him.

24/03/00 07.34 status

<u>Anita File</u>

Anita Jettison
24b Waltham Street
Chelsea
London SW3 7TH
Nat. Ins. No.   TN3280285
Nat. Health No.   426335119

Bank Account   Coutts & Co
                     440 Strand
                     London WC2R 0QS
                     591264   88712496

Store Cards   Peter Jones   £250.80
                     Fortnum & Mason   £60.21

Memberships   Hurlingham Club
                     Mark's Club
                     The Sanctuary

Credit Card   American Express [Platinum]   £3,214.70
                     3713 812345 61007 Exp. 01/01

e-mail   anitaj@saatchi-saatchi.com
password   anitaj

Quite a girl, our Anita. She lives in a fancy pad in Chelsea. Not hers, but she's paying the rent. Not many production assistants at an advertising agency have this kind of lifestyle. The money can't come from work. Like to know the company she's keeping.

Looks like she's out every night she isn't with Robert.

The cab company route worked with Robert; I try it again. Anita's cab company is making a killing out of her. Different places all over London, but not in the sorts of areas you'd expect a Chelsea girl to be hanging out. It'd be fun to map her travels for a week or two. Sketch out her movements.

When there's one drugs user in a relationship, there's probably two. Anita's got to be getting money from somewhere. And big money too. Robert's not drawing cash any more. No need to – if he's getting the stuff from Anita.

24/03/00 07.51

<u>**Anita File**</u>

MediSearch . . . accessing files Dr Miles Dobson . . .
patient: Anita Jettison
16/09/99

<u>Faxed from</u> private consulting GP to Admissions,
NHS STD Clinic, Mortimer Market, Capper Street, London WC1

Would you please see this IVDU. I have recently given her treatment for an abscess around injecting site [right arm]. She's had multiple sexual partners and is asymptomatic but I felt it was prudent for her to have a check-up, including testing for HIV and hepatitis B and C.

Just had to check out the medical records. Too many fingers pointing that way for me to ignore. And whoa, we got a live one here. Sex and drugs and rock 'n' roll all right. Just move in this here circle, where anything's allowed.

I'd say from looking at the records that Anita is seeing other people. Plural. Regular. Wouldn't you?

I'm waiting for my man . . .

A little bit of nomenclature interests me on the file. Notice she's down as an IVDU. Remember old Rob's GP referred to him as a 'drug abuser'. Subtle differences in language betray rather wider tolerances in attitudes.

One other thing. See – Anita made no attempt at any cover-up. When you go to these GU clinics you can give any goddamn name you choose and they don't ask for proof of ID or anything. If you say you're Mrs Bore, you're always Mrs Bore to them. But Anita doesn't bother. She gives her correct name – that made it even easier for me to find her.

Anita File

Vodafone You Are Here

Anita Jettison
Mobile: 07694 282 145
Account Outstanding   £349.00

Date	Time	Number	Duration
09/03	20.23	020 7229 0879	2.50 mins
	20.48	020 7229 0879	0.41 mins
	22.49	020 7588 8086	2.24 mins
12/03	19.58	020 8675 8545	1.59 mins
	20.21	020 8675 8545	1.01 mins
	23.15	020 7588 8086	2.51 mins
15/03	19.37	020 8883 2485	3.44 mins
	20.19	020 8883 2485	0.34 mins
	23.58	020 7588 8086	2.41 mins

Tel. no. called most frequently   020 7222 0423
                                    12 calls   14.3 hrs

Number Search

020 7229 0879	16 Bleakston Place SW1
020 7588 8086	ABBA Cabs SW6
020 8675 8545	26 Worcester Square SW6
020 8883 2485	4 Bethwick Crescent N6
020 7222 0423	104 Eaton Square SW1

Big mobile phone bill. She works during the day in an office, so she's got to be using that phone big time in the evening – and the night.

There's a pattern. She phones a number twice. First call lasts some minutes. Later call is very short. A couple of hours later she always calls another number, the same number. Like she's checking in or out.

I set up this neat little program. Match mobile phone numbers to addresses visited by her cab company. I get some parallels. Here's how it works: she calls. Makes an appointment. Calls again just before she arrives at the address. A while later she calls in with the central number.

It's a set-up each time.

One other item on the phone bill. She calls one number, each week. No set time or place, but never misses a week. Call lasts an hour, sometimes more. The number belongs to a Lord Wilcox Barker. Jesus! A Peer of the Realm. Oh, this is just too much to resist. The Dogg's imagination starts to run wild. What if it's phone sex! Yeah. Phone sex. Tease me, tease me.

24/03/00 07.53

Anita File

Anita Jettison

Bank Account	Coutts & Co 440 Strand London WC2R 0QS	
Account Review March 2000	591264 88712496	
Total Credits	Cash	£7,800.00
	Saatchi/Saatchi	£1,419.86
Incomings	Overseas [Banque Liechtenstein]	£6,000.00
Total Cash Withdrawals	[6 months]	£12,000.00
Notes	Max. Balance	£26,428.07
	Min. Balance	£3,214.96
	No. of days overdrawn current period	0
	ML alert. Investigated. No action required.	

Getting to Anita was easy. It's all there. On the surface. Her lifestyle, the money, the kicks.

Anita doesn't cover her trail. Makes these big payments in cash into her account each month. Doesn't seem to give a toss about paying it in without any laundry action. Notice the bank was cagey: Money Laundering alert. But nothing comes of it. Anita also gets big chunks in from an offshore account in Liechtenstein. A Liechtenstein *Anstalt*. Sophisticated, offshore money. Yet she's bringing it back into this country, waving a big red flag at the Inland Revenue. 'Come and get me, you blood suckers, you little men in worn grey suits, I'll eat you alive.'

She's out there. No cover-up. Lots to hide but she doesn't bother. A girl who's happy with her secrets.

Can you imagine it? Robert, a bit of a player himself. Bored. Got a good job but always looking for excitement. Not attached. Meets the original wild girl, and that's got to be a buzz. 'I want to suck the marrow out of life's thigh bone. Feel like I'm here on this little blue planet. I want to live. I want to live.' He's hooked up with the right girl this time. Moving out has had its benefits.

24/03/00 13.57

From: samc@riverso.co.uk
To: thedogg@acdogg.co.uk
Subject: Garden Flat, 81 Bryanston Road

I send these tasty morsels to Mr C.
  I get the message back:

> Tell me about James and Cynthia.
> Go deeper.
> Sam Collier

<u>**Cynthia File**</u>

MORI Newsletter

RESEARCH WITH RESPONSIBILITY
BY C. SHEPHERD

JUNE 1999

So I think it is vital that corporations devote time and attention to the notion of privacy. They will need to develop the ideas of awareness (I know that this data will be used), and what I have called 'voluntary surrender' (I am happy to give you this data), and 'conditional guarantee' (on these terms only). These are the future ground rules of responsible research and will need to be spelt out clearly and overtly, not hidden in small print . . .

Boots the Chemist Ltd
Hays Galleria
London SE1
27/03/00

Clairol Herbal Essence	£4.38
BIC Sensitive razors 12-pack	£2.59
Total	£6.97
Paid	VISA
Ms C. Shepherd	4550 9698 1291 7461 Exp. 03/01
Boots Advantage Card	492148986
Previous pts total	1243
Pts awarded	23
New pts total	1266

What about Cynthia?

I wonder what Cynthia would think of me. We're sort of in the same line of business, after all. I've looked up her report, 'Research with Responsibility'. [Interesting reading – like she's saying, 'Trust me. Give me your facts. I won't tell anyone else about them, I won't betray you . . .'] She doesn't get it yet. She doesn't really get what's going on. What if I met her one day, maybe at some research seminar. We'd get to talking. I'd mention casually that I had read her paper. Flatter the girl. Dogg, you dog.

Then I'd hit her with the facts.

Cynthia, there is no privacy. I repeat. We have reached the end of privacy. If I want to know your parents' telephone number, all I have to do is check out the Friends and Family account with your telecoms provider. More personal? OK: you shave your legs in the bath, Cynthia. It's a guess. But I do know that last week you bought a 12-pack of disposable BIC razors from Boots, but no shaving foam. So you shave your legs and they're already wet. Some smart-arse will say maybe she shaves her legs in the basin, in the shower, etc., etc. Fine. That's not the point. The point is I can get real close to Cynthia with nothing more than a shopping list. A shopping list is a lens. Put all the lenses together and you've got a telescope into every corner of her life.

There is no privacy. Lace curtains twitch in the global village and the hand behind them is yours. Information wants to be free. You've set it free. We're all in the know now.

06/04/00 14.22

Cynthia File

Virgin Megastores
Kings Walk Mall
122 Kings Road
London SW3
01/04/00

Carly Simon, *Greatest Hits*	£12.99
Mary Chapin Carpenter, *Shooting Straight in the Dark*	£13.99
Total	£26.98
Paid	VISA
Ms C. Shepherd	4550 9698 1291 7461 Exp. 03/01

So you see, Cynthia, I don't need to meet you. I already have, on file. I know about you.

If I met you, in person, would I know you any better? You'd tell me stuff about yourself. But you'd tell me what you want me to know. You'd filter and select. You'd build a picture that *you* think is true.

If I met you in an on-line chat room, you'd do the same. Filter and select.

But my file is the true you. Intimate information.

That's the trouble. All this time I've been thinking: stick to the facts, Dogg, and you can't get involved. But that's not true. Facts are the basis for intimacy. The more you know about someone, the better you know them, the more you get drawn in. You get a liking for it.

13/04/00 04.25 status

James File

Selfridges Store Account
08/04/00

Beauty Department
Chanel No. 5 Parfum   £54.00
Total   £54.00

Paid   Acct No.
Mr J. Cameron   3376 48 7452 9762 3148 Exp. 04/01

Oddbins
Great Portland Street
London W1

Wine
Perrier Jouet Millésime   £35.99

Paid   Lloyds Mcard
Mr J. Cameron   4775 9180 2227 4176 Exp. 12/00

Cynthia File

Boots the Chemist Ltd
290 Oxford Street
London W1
01/04/00

Dove Beauty   £2.19
Tampax 32   £3.05
Macleans Extra White   £2.09
Toothbrushes 2 @ £1.49   £2.98
Sure for Men   £3.30
Total   £13.61

Paid   VISA
Ms C. Shepherd   4550 9698 1291 7461 Exp. 03/01

Boots Advantage Card   492148986
Previous pts total   1266
Pts awarded   50
New pts total   1316

The boyfriend James is a romantic. No doubt about it. Bet if he sent a Valentine's message, he'd sign himself 'Bear'. Buys Chanel No. 5. Now, James probably 'knows' that Chanel No. 5 is Cynthia's perfume. Just could be though that it's his idea of what she should wear. Classically feminine. Does that sound like our idealist researcher with an anthropology degree and an attitude list as long as your arm? More like James is projecting his image of the ideal woman onto Cynthia.

He buys perfume, not eau de toilette. If this was a casual purchase, he would have bought her eau de toilette. But he goes for the smaller bottle. Perfume is like magic dust. Dab a little behind the ear, and you will be transformed, like someone said: 'I don't sell cosmetics, I sell hope.' People don't buy perfume to smell different but to be different. The giver, to transform.

Cynthia has been doing some spending in the cosmetics department too. Along with her usual list of necessities, she's bought some male deodorant. For James. Getting to know you, getting to like the things you do. Here we are, back on the edge of the holy grail of couple status: the kit on the bathroom shelf. Intimacy in bottles and tubes. James and Cynthia are really getting on.

I pick out the purchase of Chanel No. 5. It caught my eye. Was this a defining moment, a measure of their intimacy? A butterfly flaps its wings in Brazil and causes a hurricane in China. That's Chaos for you. In the chaos of human relationships, in the making of partnerships, can we watch the butterfly flap its wings, can we distinguish the barely seen gesture? Can we identify that right word spoken at the right time; the courteous act; the betrayal of passion in an unlikely remark; the moment when the world stopped for this particular couple, and they hopped onto the same orbit?

Yes, if we look closely enough.

Emmanuelle

THE CLUB MAGAZINE FOR WOMEN WITH
A SENSE OF ADVENTURE

Private Member Subscription Only

Sex 2000 Survey: What our readers really think

Millennium Hedonism. Everyone's doing it.

FREE PRIZE DRAW: One Year's Free Subscription

Worrying, isn't it, how close I can get to these two people? Yet they don't even know that I exist. I know more about them than their closest friends. I am intimate with them while they are ignorant of me.

I can tell you how they have sex.

I can even get into bed with our Cynthia.

She's filled in one of those sex surveys, in a mag called *Emmanuelle* she gets on private subscription; membership stuff. But, however private, the mag still has a database. All I had to do was go through the responses to recent surveys, extract the simple scramble, and Dogg gets a printout of what Cynthia says.

Do you want to turn the page?

Emmanuelle

MAY 2000

SEX 2000 SURVEY

Respondent: C. Shepherd, 81 Bryanston Road, NW6 8KR

	YES	NO
Are you currently in a sexual relationship?	0	
Have you shared all your past sexual experiences with your current partner?		0
Does he tell you about his past?		0
Are there things you would not tell your partner?	0	
Have you ever been raped or subjected to sexual assault?	0	
Did you know the attacker?	0	
Do you consider yourself capable of violence in matters of love or passion?		0

Please give your answers to/views on the following in the box provided.

What's your favourite sexual position?

XXXXXXXXXXXXXXX

How many sexual partners have you had?

XXXXXXX

Do you approve of one-night stands?

XXXXXXXXXXXXXXXXXXXXXXXXXXXXXXXXXXX

Do you enjoy oral sex?

XXXXXXXXXXXXXXXXXXXXXXXXXXXXXXXXXXXXXXXXXXX

Have you ever had sex with a married man/woman?

XXXXXX

Do you have lesbian fantasies? If so, describe:

XXXXXXXXXXXXXXXXXXXXXXXXXXXXXXXXXXXXXXXXXXXXXX

Describe your most complete/satisfying sexual experience to date:

XXXXXXXXXXXXXXXXXXXXXXXXXXXXXXXXXXXXXXXXXXXXXXXXXXXXX

She's pretty straight; admits that she doesn't tell her partner about all her past experiences. Admits to the publisher, though not to her partner, that she's been the victim of a rape. Does the publisher want to know? You bet.

Why does she tell a publisher – and me – more than she tells her lover? She could have been lured into it by the prize. But our Cynthia's not that avaricious. Maybe she responds out of professional interest. The researcher researched. Could be a neat little irony that appeals to her. Or maybe it's the thrill of making answers in the dark. In a room where no-one can hear, you finally spill the beans. You can't go on with this secret inside you. There's an unbearable desire to talk. To any-one, or anything.

So, in the safety of a questionnaire, she feels her dark secret is being projected onto black walls, an image on obscurity. She runs her hands over the invisible words on the wall. She feels better, just knowing the words are there. Anonymous graffiti. (The same way that all graffiti satisfies through anonymous unburdening.) But she's not anonymous. She's known. Her secret ramblings are overheard, stored, available.

The Dogg could reveal more: how she feels about oral sex. Her favourite position. Her lesbian fantasy. Her most complete sexual ex-perience. All her intimacies. I will not tell you these things. Do you want to know; do you want to know the things I leave out, more than the things I tell you about? Do you want to know more? If you were Dogg, where would you stop?

THE MEDIUM IS THE MESSAGE

MARSHALL MCLUHAN

Herbert Marshall McLuhan. With telephone and TV it is not so much the message as the sender that is 'sent'. Marshall . . .

I need a break.

Time to reflect. Wonder about the world I'm moving into. This case is taking me into the real-real electronic world, blurring the distinctions for me between what's on-line and what's off-line. The parallel lines are coming together.

I'm no longer looking at facts. I'm starting to feel the facts.

And it's breathtaking. I'm as high as Marshall McLuhan when he said: 'Ours is a brand-new world of allatonceness. Time has ceased, space has vanished . . . we live in a simultaneous happening.' Yeah, I'm living it, Marshall. I'm in the simultaneous happening. I'm living in @, where the tenses have got all mixed up in the data slipstream. I live in the permanent now, where the past is always present, because the data is always present. No delete button. Nothing can ever be truly erased. e-mail never dies.

Data exists in a timeless present. Data is the present. It is the now. Collect it and you find another self.

You are not just you. You are out there. You exist on a decentralized database.

You are in @.

Simultaneously.

Allatonce.

Forever.

Better get used to it, baby.

THE LIST OF ALL BOTS

Bot Design
Chatter Bots
Commerce Bots
Data Mining Bots
E-Mail Bots
Fun Bots
Game Bots
Government Bots
Knowledge Bots
Misc. Bots
News Bots
Newsgroup Bots
Research on Bots
Search Bots
Shopping Bots
Software Bots
Stock Bots
Update Bots
Web Development

Don't miss: The Best of Bots

That's the good side of it.

But there's another side. Something I have to figure out for myself: the parallel lines coming together. I'm getting involved in this case. I'm taking it personally.

It makes me feel like I'm a voyeur. Because I'm not just doing all this for professional reasons. If I'm honest, I want to get closer. Personally.

I'm getting to know these characters so well. Be intimate with them. I'm crossing over. From my world into theirs.

If you exist in @ you've got to keep your detachment, otherwise you'll only get downed in the cross-fire. Get drawn into the messy world of human decisions, where there are no absolutes, no right answers, only degrees of wrongness.

If I have learnt anything in the past weeks it is this: you can push the technology to its limits and keep on pushing. But sooner or later you'll find that the real limit is you. The barrier is how much you can take before you break, and cross over.

James File
Cynthia File

BA Ticketing
21/04/00

BA 586 LHR VCE	dep. 20.00	arr. 23.00
BA 587 VCE LHR	dep. 12.55	arr. 14.05
Travellers:	Mr James Cameron	
	Ms Cynthia Shepherd	
Econ. Full Fare x 2	£310.00	
Paid	Lloyds Mcard	
Mr J. Cameron	4775 9180 2227 4176 Exp. 12/00	

Hotel La Bellezza
Venice
**** Star
21/04/00

Room 46: Prepaid
Double

Extras		
Mbar	Lira	6,400.00
Room Service	Lira	16,000.00
Mbar	Lira	38,400.00
Mbar	Lira	6,400.00
Breakfast	Lira	54,400.00
Room Service	Lira	8,000.00
Breakfast	Lira	54,400.00
Total	Lira	184,000.00

Paid	Lloyds Mcard
Mr J. Cameron	4775 9180 2227 4176 Exp. 12/00

James and Cynthia are on a plane. Off to Venice for the weekend. From the booking it looks like a last-minute thing: spur of the moment. James, the romantic. But it always beats Dogg why couples go to Venice for this sort of fling. Shows a lack of imagination if you ask Dogg.

They choose a smart hotel with views of the Grand Canal. The bill checks out; everything you'd expect from a romantic weekend. Lots of minibar. Breakfast in the room on both mornings. Room service on the first night.

They arrive. Throw open the shutters. Look out from the balcony. He stands beside her. They kiss. Lightly. She runs her hands up his chest. He kisses her neck. Her eyelids. Her lips. The window is open. Warm night air. All things forgotten. Only the moment.

Only not all things are forgotten. Nothing is deleted. As they make love on the small armchair, beside an open window, on a warm Venetian night, does she think of other times?

James File

Waterstone's Heathrow Branch
21/04/00
Venice for Pleasure
by J. G. Links   £12.95

Paid   Lloyds Mcard
Mr J. Cameron   4775 9180 2227 4176 Exp. 12/00

Venice Weather

Sunny
Temperature 20°

Moda Maffeo Leon
22/04/00
Jacket   Lira 779,500.00

Paid   Lloyds Mcard
Mr J. Cameron   4775 9180 2227 4176 Exp. 12/00

Murano Glass
22/04/00
6 x Goblets   Lira 540,000.00

Paid   Lloyds Mcard
Mr J. Cameron   4775 9180 2227 4176 Exp. 12/00

Cynthia File

Moda Maffeo Leon
22/04/00
Briefcase   Lira 561,240.00

Paid   VISA
Ms C. Shepherd   4550 9698 1291 7461 Exp. 03/01

I don't have to be left behind. If I want to, I can go anywhere. I can watch snow falling on Red Square. I can watch the surf on Malibu. Simultaneous happenings, seen simultaneously. All it takes is a webcam. @ isn't just timeless, it's boundless too.

Right now, for example, I could be there with James and Cynthia in Venice. Emotionally, electronically. Makes me wonder whether it's being there or going there that matters. And what does going 'there' mean; just a voyeur voyage?

They had breakfast in their room on the first morning. Coffee, bread, jam and croissants. From their balcony, they look across the Grand Canal and catch a glimpse of the Rialto Bridge.

They leave the hotel some time before 11.00, because he buys her an expensive sheepskin coat, the sort much beloved by Venetians for cold winter nights, from the Moda Maffeo Leon; VISA authorization at 11.12. The Moda Maffeo Leon is on the Campiello del Remer, a few minutes' walk from their hotel. But Cynthia isn't the impulsive type, she would have browsed around the shop first, tried on several different coats before selecting one. So my guess is that they probably left by 10.30 at the latest. At the same shop Cynthia buys a leather briefcase. Our Prada girl with a leather briefcase? Much more likely a present for him.

I'm there with them. I can access the same guidebook that James bought before from Waterstone's at Heathrow. Like them, I read that the four horses of St Mark's started out in Greece, turned up on Trajan's Arch in Rome, then went to Constantinople, from where they were looted by the Venetians during the Fourth Crusade. I walk with James and Cynthia down the Strada Nova, past Corte Seconda del Milione [named after Marco Polo's book of travels], onto Rio dei Miracoli, before crossing the Ponte de l'Ogio [ogio means oil].

They stop again at the Galleria dell' Commedia. They buy masks, presumably like the ones Venetians wear at Carnival. Ideal presents or sitting-room wall memorabilia. They lunch at Do Forni, safe choice. In the afternoon they take a vaporetto to Murano and watch the blowers turn liquid into glass. They buy six goblets. Return to the hotel; tea in the lobby. Dinner at Da Nane Mora.

James File

Ristorante Vecia Cavanna
Venezia
Italia
23/04/00

1 x Prosecco
1 x Vitello [Scaloppine]
1 x Linguine
2 x Insalata
2 x Café
Total   Lira 521,830.00

Paid   Lloyds Mcard
Mr J. Cameron   4775 9180 2227 4176 Exp. 12/00
                                  Auth. 15:15

Ristorante Locanda Montin
Venezia
Italia
23/04/00

Total   Lira 514,460.00

Paid   Lloyds Mcard
Mr J. Cameron   4775 9180 2227 4176 Exp. 12/00
                                  Auth. 22.45

Next day, James and Cynthia lunch at the Vecia Cavanna. One of the best in Venice. They eat black shrimps, one veal cutlet and one spaghetti al pomodoro, accompanied by a bottle of Prosecco. Two coffees. They move on, buying books at the Libreria del Piazza, just off St Mark's. Another coffee, this time at Florian's. Maybe some cash shopping in between; take the lift up the Campanile for the best view of the city, but interestingly you can't see a single canal.

A long afternoon walk along the Zattere. Slow wonder in Levant light. Back to the hotel; room service drinks at 7.43. Dinner at Locanda Montin, busy, the top garden restaurant in Venice. All they needed for the perfect final day in Venice was a drink at Harry's Bar. I would have taken Cynthia to Harry's Bar, James. So why didn't they drop by? It serves the best dry Martinis in the universe [made with dry white wine, not vermouth] and sleek little sandwiches with the crusts cut off. I can almost taste the Martini.

Cynthia File

VISA
Ms C. Shepherd
Card No. 4550 9698 1291 7461 Exp. 03/01

Search Criteria: match all payments by Visa Card 4550 9698 1291 7461 with payments having Italy paycode [IL].

22/10/92	Hotel Rialto, Venezia	
	Room	Lira 230,000.00
22/10/92	Harry's Bar	Lira 16,000.00
23/10/92	Artigianato San Marco	Lira 24,000.00

Search flights match Italy 20–22/10/92 BA/British Midland/Alitalia with Ms C. Shepherd

Searching . . .

Alitalia
21/10/92

Flight 244
Ms C. Shepherd
Seat 34b
Paid   VISA
Mr A. Hocking   4771 1664 9800 7421 Exp. 09/93

Restaurant bills don't lie; nor do bar tabs. Take a look at this one from Harry's Bar in Venice. A certain Ms C. Shepherd paid for it with her VISA card – that's how the Dogg came to dig it up. Cynthia visited Harry's Bar on her first trip to Venice. And she wasn't alone. She slept in a small hotel. Not on the Grand Canal, more of the backpackers' territory. She travelled by Alitalia – her ticket paid for by Mr Andrew Hocking. She, or rather they, stayed three nights in Venice.

Cynthia File

COUNTY COURT FILES

Name Search . . . Andrew Hocking

256 items

Match against Ms C. Shepherd

1 Match:

Court date	20/04/93
Case number	6704811
Court name	Hackney
Action brought by	Ms Cynthia Jane Shepherd
Case status	Dismissed 20/04/93
Court date	20/04/93
Case number	6704811
Court name	Hackney
Defendant	Mr A. Hocking
Case status	Dismissed 20/04/93

I check the name Andrew Hocking against court files. He was the defendant in an action not long after the visit to Venice. It was a rape case. The plaintiff, a Ms C. Shepherd.

Well, Cynthia, Prada girl. The past truly is retrievable, eternally present, to anyone. The Dogg deduces: you go on holiday, things don't work out. You row. Mr Hocking is not the man for you. You come back to the UK and break off the relationship. A tearful meeting after work. Only Mr Hocking decides he'll have one last go at changing your mind. Maybe he turns up at your flat unannounced one evening, says he just wants to talk. Try to sort things out. You let him in. Who knows what happens next, Cynthia? A couple of drinks; a struggle in the sitting room. Do you remember? Yes, every detail. Just like you explained to the police and then to Rape Crisis. Just like you explained in court. He ties you up. Gags you. Rapes you. You recounted the details over and over again. Only that wasn't enough. It was his word against yours. You knew him; he was your ex. You liked to play games: get tied up. All very troublesome to your case. Difficult to know whom we should believe. Could be Andrew was innocent; maybe he broke off the relationship with you, Cynthia. And you were so upset, you couldn't handle it. Wanted revenge: public, damaging, nasty revenge. That's another story.

So, if you told James about all this now, would it make any difference? Would he love you any less? What information, when: that's the big ticket. If James had known about Cynthia's past when they first met, would that have made any difference? Probably not. But if he found out now, how would that change things? What information, when. It's the *when* that fascinates the Dogg. The information is always present, always there, yet timed at the moment of its release. Facts don't change in themselves but are modified by time. Maybe the when is more important than what. The same facts in a different order, different story.

UK REGISTER OF ELECTORS

Mr Andrew Hocking
17 Cranleigh Gardens
London SW6 5TY

One more item. Mr Andrew Hocking lives at 17 Cranleigh Gardens, a few doors down from Robert. Coincidence? There are too many coincidences in this world, that's what the Dogg says. Perhaps they even know one another, say good morning occasionally on the walk to the tube or in the local newsagent's.

You might say that whether Robert knows Andrew depends on chance. Just as it's pure chance that they live in the same street. You're right, but only up to a point. The data says that certain streets in certain areas are far more likely to house young professionals than others. So the fact that Robert and Andrew have both selected the same locale isn't as much of a coincidence as it seems.

Hillary Clinton once said, as a kind of character reference for Bill, 'My husband has never met a stranger.' Prophetic words, Hills baby. Hills meant that old Bill is so warm to people that everyone feels on first meeting they've known him for ever. Prophetic, Hills, because tomorrow we may never meet a stranger again.

You see, when it comes to these two guys Robert and Andrew knowing each other, right now that depends on happenstance. But you could find out who lives in your street. No difficulty in that, anyone could. It's just that the Dogg is a bit ahead of the pack, a professional in these matters.

30/4/00 13.35 status

James File

Austin Reed Store Account
James Cameron
Acct No. 022C117219 Exp. 04/02
No transactions in last 3 months

**Ralph Lauren
1 New Bond Street
London W1**

Shirt	£79.50
Shirt	£60.00
Jacket	£320.00
Knitwear	£115.00
Total	£574.50

Paid	Lloyds Mcard
Mr J. Cameron	4775 9180 2227 4176 Exp. 12/00

**Sainsbury's
17 Camden Road
London NW1
Making Life Taste Better
06/05/00**

Crespo Grn Olive/Pimento 907 g	£1.99
Häagen-Dazs Caramel 500 ml	£3.69
Häagen-Dazs Cookies & Cream 500 ml	£3.69
B&J Fudge Brownie 500 ml	£3.69
Kettle Chip Slt&Vn	£1.45
Kettle Chip Cheddar	£1.45
Total	£15.96

Paid	Lloyds Mcard
Mr J. Cameron	4775 9180 2227 4176 Exp. 12/00

Sky Digital
amended 13/05/00

James Cameron/Cynthia Shepherd	Acct No. 000456 334 65
Sky World [Sky MovieMax, Sky Cinema]	£29.99
Film Four	£5.99

In London, James and Cynthia are getting closer. The subtlest of changes showing up in their pattern. Changes that the Dogg is programmed to notice.

For instance, James hasn't used his Austin Reed store card in months. Not a great clothes man, one surmises. But now he's spending money on gear not from Austin Reed, but Ralph Lauren. He's buying up. Over £500 in one visit. Dressing for her. Taking them both to a new level: the professional couple. Today you can do that with the brands you buy. You don't have to wait two generations to be accepted any more. It's much more democratic. You can do it in an afternoon.

Why should this matter? Am I getting too fancy, reading too much into all this? Does the move from one brand to another illuminate the passage of the spirit in its eternal quest for self-fulfilment? Not exactly. But the move definitely does signal psychological change. By filling in the space between two brands I can measure the state of mind.

I am getting closer to their nowness.

Same with the groceries. Compare the stuff they're buying from Sainsbury's now to the items they used to buy even a few weeks ago and you'll see some interesting additions. Real coffee. Häagen-Dazs. Designer crisps. Stuffed olives. Who the hell actually likes stuffed olives? It's all party food. The humour in the home is happier. No longer just rushing back, changing and out to meet friends. They're spending time together in. Treating one another. Peeling grapes in the twilight.

The Sky package has changed too. Movies. We get the picture: sitting on the sofa; content with one another's company. Data is a state of mind.

James File

Lord's
The Home of Cricket ·
18/05/00

1st Cornhill Test Match
England vs Zimbabwe

Corporate Hospitality Suite No. 326
Arthur Andersen Entertaining

Breakdown of costs:
Wines, etc. 19/05/00   £410.00
Wines, etc. 20/05/00   £930.00

20/05/00–27/08/00
Glyndebourne Festival Opera
Corporate Sponsors
A. Andersen

Cynthia File

Counselling and Psychotherapy Partnership
20/05/00

Appt 2.00–2.50   £110.00

Paid   VISA
Ms C. Shepherd   4550 9698 1291 7461 Exp. 03/01

Simultaneous happenings. Seen simultaneously. Strange how that throws up the unexpected. On Saturday 20 May, James attends the Test Match at Lord's. Nothing unexpected in that. His firm has a suite for corporate entertaining. Please note the levels of spending on different days. Very different. On the nineteenth they serve up wine at £9.00 per bottle. On the twentieth, it's champagne at £28.95. I'd say we have a classic A and B list situation working here. When the firm wants to impress the important clients out comes the champagne; for the other Charlies it's the white Burgundy. Oh, the world of business is full of such delicate nuance. Perhaps that's why they like going to Glyndebourne so much.

The same afternoon Cynthia makes a new payment: £110 to the Counselling and Psychotherapy Partnership, an upmarket counselling outfit just off Harley Street. Their site on the Web lists anxiety, stress, depression, panic, psychosexual and relationships. I could access Cynthia's files if I wanted to. But that's not necessary. It's clear to me what she went for. Dogg can sniff it a mile off.

Somehow I don't get the feeling that Cynthia has told James about her past. Why sneak out to a counselling session while James is at Lord's? More crucially, why agree to go to Venice? Try this scenario: James the romantic chose it as the ideal destination for a happy couple of days. Cynthia was upset about something. She'd just been done for speeding. Why not take a couple of days' break, to cheer her up? That's how I see it playing. She says that would be lovely, where are we going? Ah, says James, it's a surprise. All you need to do is pack for a couple of days. Some smart gear but mostly casual. Cynthia is happy and excited. They get to Heathrow. The tickets finally come out: they're going to Venice. The last place on earth that Cynthia would have chosen. Bad scene all round. The trip to Venice has opened old wounds. Being with James makes them more difficult to cope with. He goes to the cricket. She goes for counselling.

She's cracking.

e-mail log thedogg@acdogg.co.uk

James File

John Lewis Store Account
18/05/00

Acct No. 9761 89412 Exp. 08/02

Zeiss Binocs	£265.00
829.80302	
Total	£265.00

Paid	Acct No.
Mr J. Cameron	9761 89412 Exp. 08/02

Unexpected. Departing from his usual reticence, Mr C sends me a note unprompted:

> Time is running out, Dogg.

Not sure what I should make of this. Mr C has never mentioned timetables before.

The barely audible sound of a clock, down the corridor, at the end of the hall. Out of sight. Running down unnoticed.

23/05/00 11.15

<u>**James File**</u>

<u>**Opening DOGG File**</u>

jamesc@aandersen.co.uk
Lotus Notes

Match entries/deleted entries to 'Rob', 'Robbo', Robert', 'Robert Bolton'
01/03/00 to date . , .

14/03	lunch Rob	entered 02/03 deleted 13/03
30/03	drinks Robbo	entered 13/03 deleted 30/03
07/04	drinks Robbo	entered 20/03 deleted 07/04
17/04	drinks Robert	entered 07/04 deleted 17/04
26/05	lunch Robert	

All three characters have secrets. A weakness. It's only a matter of time before they crack. And when they do – and I suspect all three will have to crack first – then I'll know what all this deal with Mr C is about. Right now I can't tell which way this job is going.

Are these characters going to change one another's story?

They are already.

Cynthia and James are moving closer together; James and Robert are drifting apart.

Take a look into James's diary. Several proposed meets with Robert have been cancelled; one lunch date fixed in a few weeks' time.

Is James going to crack? No signs yet.

James File

Employee Appraisal Form

UPDATES 01/05/00, DEPARTMENT 8E

JAMES CAMERON

Overall Grade: Excellent

Shows a high degree of trustworthiness and empathy. Of particular note is his disclosure of a hitherto unnoticed critical lapse of judgement with regard to tax-sensitive client information. This voluntary disclosure facilitated coaching and development of a genuinely promising junior member. To reveal this information at a time when he is being considered for partnership is to be particularly commended.

PERSONAL NOTES

James's sympathetic handling of and support for his secretary who has been performing poorly as a consequence of domestic stress indicates a particular sensitivity.

Like Dogg, James is a trusting soul. He's also trustworthy. Two little bits of info from his personal files at Arthur Andersen prove the point.

First, looks like just when he's coming up for election to partnership, he blows the gaff on some past misdemeanour. In fact, the crime was nothing too sinister; but withholding the information would have been much more serious. James got into a spot of bother with a client. He erased a bit of information from a client file. He didn't think anything of it at the time, just clearing out old details. A few months later the tax narks come snooping and they can't find what they're after. 'Where is it, old son?' they say. Only of course tax narks don't talk like that any more. They're much too refined and snide now. Never let the tax boys start tootling with your files. They're as bad as the Dogg. And that's bad. Anyway, James reinstates the information, client gets collared but the narks are happy. Happy all round, except for the client, and except for the fact that no-one else at the firm knows about this.

James knows that sooner or later the information may come to light. It's a gamble. Should he tell his bosses or not? He chooses the honourable path and owns up. [Maybe he's learnt from that Animal Rights incident; carried the guilt with him and doesn't want another secret.] Instead of sacking him on the spot, the bosses are impressed. Anyone can make a mistake, but you went much further, James. You gave up the information freely. That's why you got commended for it. Just goes to prove Dogg's motto. Give up the data freely, because whatever you have to hide will be found in the end. No hiding place now, inside or outside the kennel.

The second item of note on his file concerns another woman. His secretary Jane in fact. Seems she got into marital bother, or 'domestic stress' as it's coded on the file. Her husband – you know, the one who promised to love and protect her – probably starts to beat her up. Turns up at the office with a big, bad bruise. Knocked herself on the cupboard door. You know the sort of thing. Jane starts to go loopy; files go missing; she can't get the job done. James spots there's something amiss and offers help. Sensitive soul, our James. For a bloke, that is.

THE REIKI PAGE

Reiki [pronounced ray-key] is a method of natural healing based on the application of Universal Life Force Energy (the name literally means Universal Life Force Energy).

Just for today, do not worry.
Just for today, do not anger.
Honor your parents, teachers, and elders.
Earn your living honestly.
Show gratitude to everything.

Dr Mikao Usui

Imagine the implications of the universe around us made from energy which can be shaped and manipulated by thoughts.

Check out James's reading. On the spiritual side. And that Reiki week-end he went to a while back? It wasn't a business event. It's one of these spiritual get-togethers.

James is looking for the perennial philosophy.

I wonder why.

24/05/00 03.15

James File

**MediSearch . . . accessing files Dr William Arbuthnot . . .
patient: James Cameron**

Patient History

1. Undescended testicles, not noticed until 10/11 yrs. Corrected by bilateral orchidopexy. Aware of increased risk of testicular cancer. No symptoms. Testing procedure explained . . .

With a medical history like this, is it that surprising that James is out there searching for some Greater Truth? I mean, if you were a bloke who had that kind of problem, wouldn't you? But this is tricky ground: we could assign all sorts of behaviour and motives to this single fact that would just be supposition. We'd be making up a lot of baggage for James that he simply may not carry.

And that's my beef with loads of things that happened in the old twentieth C. It was a century obsessed with taking one small personal detail and explaining the person's whole life as a consequence of it. Mr Freud invented the twentieth C. He made writers go mad and critics go crazy. [Jesus, most of them would have written whole books about this one little instance – how James agonized over it, how it twisted him, made him shut out the world, vulnerable, etc., etc. . . . and other garbage.] Whole generations getting off on making connections that may never have been there. That's something that's going to change in the twenty-first C.

Don't explain a person by a single fact. It's the pattern that's them.

Anyway, this kind of operation isn't all that uncommon. It's just that it's rarely talked about on a mates' night out down the pub. Side effects: a scar on the scrotum and smaller testicles. Doubts about its effect on fertility, but nothing certain. You can just hear the doctor uttering those comforting words: 'Get on with your life. Don't worry about it.'

Robert File

robbo@saatchi-saatchi.com

Last ten website visits >>>

1.	www.sweetpain.com	25.06 mins
2.	www.afetish.com	31.56 mins
3.	www.scrum.com	3.41 mins
4.	www.genealogy.com	42.16 mins
5.	www.familysearch.org	23.56 mins
6.	www.genealogytoolbox.com	12.45 mins
7.	www.bondage.com	46.23 mins
8.	www.lastminute.com	5.51 mins
9.	www.ancestry.com	36.06 mins
10.	www.easyart.com	7.47 mins

ancestry.com

THE BEST PLACE TO FIND YOUR ANCESTORS

SEARCH 400 MILLION NAMES IN 1,806 DATABASES

robbo@saatchi-saatchi.com
Last 5 requests on google.com >>>
1.   reaperbot
2.   genealogy
3.   family history
4.   find a person
5.   hidden identity

For the past couple of weeks the Dogg has had a track on Robert's Internet usage – just a precaution. In fact, it's the first thing any pro will do on a case, put on an Internet tail just to see what flotsam gets thrown up on the wake. As I keep advising clients, 'Every time you go in to the Net, you leave a trail a mile wide.' Now, most people are either in there making visitations for the sex or for health. One third of Internet hits are related to health matters, self-diagnosis, patient heal thyself, the Net as your desktop quack. Presumably the other two-thirds of users are into cyberbondage.com. Like Robert. Robbo takes in a little visit to the land of ropes and shiny leather, before he goes to that other great Internet growth industry: genealogy.

Robert spends an average of forty minutes in four different genealogy sites. He's looking for something. This is how it goes: he taps in 'genealogy' into a search engine and a few seconds later – wham, he's got all this juicy material. Makes him, like everyone else, feel power-ful. Instantly informed. Then it takes him hours of wading through half-relevant stuff to realize he doesn't know enough to make the search process work. Frustration.

My bet is that he finds nothing, because his searches change from genealogy to the 'find a person' directories. He's looking for someone.

Anita File

<u>Deed Poll Records</u>

Changes: to surnames
25/08/93

Anita Katherine Jettison   b. 23/08/72
Previous Name   Anita Katherine Wilcox Barker

Father   Geoffrey Wilcox Barker
Mother   Serena Wilcox Barker [d. 18/06/86]

Genealogy, family history, that unstinting desire to know from whence we came. To know who we are through the web of descent. It does not interest the Dogg. I am living in the now. I am who I am. I do what I do.

If I have a use for the past, it is only in what it reveals about the present. Others just want the past for its own sake. When the Mormons opened up their family history database to all, they had a zillion hits on the first day. What is going on? The global village using the most powerful knowledge tool mankind has made – for what? To check out where Grandpa was born.

But it's an interesting detail, a break in Robert's pattern. All things are potentially useful, precious; in the gloom of the mine there will always lie the diamond. Whose past is Robert checking out? Anita, Cynthia or James? The Dogg has hit on Cynthia's and James's families. Nothing interesting there. But there's still a lot to learn about Anita.

I start Robert's search again, but in a different place. Anita Jettison.

Name changed by deed poll.

Anita is not Anita.

Anita Jettison – our wide-eyed wild child, our girl with no secrets – has a past she wants to forget or deny. Anita is an aristo. Born of the Wilcox Barkers. In *Debrett's*. Coat of arms with lions rampant, no doubt.

So Robert's a pretty savvy guy. Likes to get the info on people, like I do. Wants to know who he's dating. I'd guess he could see a mile off that there was more to Anita than Miss Production Assistant. The accent, far too posh. The clothes. Just the odd suit that gave things away. Maybe she made some reference to another world – like Royal Ascot. And besides, she seems loaded with cash. It got him thinking. She talks posh. Fancy flat. Has the money for his drugs, yet she's a production assistant at Saatchis'. It doesn't compute to Robert. He starts looking.

24/05/00 14.51 status

<u>Anita File</u>

Anita Katherine Wilcox Barker

Bank Account	Coutts & Co.
	440 Strand
	London WC2 0QS
	591264 88712496

Monthly Credit   Banque Liechtenstein: Wilcox Barker Family
Trust. A & M.   £6,000.00

Browns
South Molton Street
London W1
16/05/99

Jil Sander Suit	£1,000.00
Jil Sander Shoes	£250.00
Total	£1,250.00

Paid	AMEX
Ms A. Jettison	3713 812345 61007 Exp. 01/01

It didn't compute for me either.

I have made a mistake. I got too carried away with Anita's lifestyle. I liked the way she too lived in the now. The fact that she breathed on the surface, seemed to have no secrets, that threw me. Her openness was her best defence. Or maybe she thought: get caught for the smaller lie to hide the bigger one.

The bigger lie was her name.

Lord Wilcox Barker. The guy she phones once a week is her father, not some old pervert in a studded leather armchair getting off on phone sex. He's a widower. Anita's mother died young; when Anita was just fourteen.

And that money from Liechtenstein. I should have got that straight off. Follow the money: except you followed the wrong money, Dogg; you followed the sexy money. The money from abroad is trust money.

Anita, our wild child, is a trustafarian. She has the past to abuse her present.

26/05/00 02.56

<u>DOGG File</u>

INVESTIGATIONS:

<u>Barclays Online</u>
<u>Invest Communicator</u>
<u>Digital Animation</u>
<u>81 Bryanston Road</u>
<u>HMV – Staff</u>
<u>HMV – Management</u>
<u>Iceland</u>
<u>Stepstone</u>
<u>Virgin Airlines</u>
<u>Lucas Alexander Whitley</u>
<u>Hodder & Stoughton</u>
<u>17 Philpott Street</u>
<u>Inland Revenue</u>
<u>Du Pont Corporation</u>

The message goes out to Mr C. Update on the Bryanston Road Three:

> Robert has moved out and started up with a new girlfriend, Anita. Anita is the Action: money, drugs, 'now life'. The 'me generation' in a svelte capsule. Only she's been covering her past.

> James and Cynthia are getting closer. Going on romantic breaks. Buying one another bathroom brands. James is hard-working, appears honest. Cynthia is screwed up. And a little deceitful. She hasn't told James about the rape. And she didn't tell James she had been to Venice before. How would that have made him feel; knowing that the one he loves is hiding such an experience? That she has loved in Venice on another night, with another. Nothing unusual in Cynthia having a past, except that knowing about her past would have modified James's feelings. For a start he probably wouldn't have chosen Venice. Suppose it all stacks up: Cynthia is 'Research with Responsibility'. Keeping things secret. The privacy girl.

I get no reply from Mr C.

Cynthia File

MediSearch . . . accessing files Dr Gavin Richardson . . .
patient: Ms C. Shepherd

NO. 247712685

09/11/99

Pill Repeat. Well. Happy with Pill. No Problems. BP 120/70. M: Microgynon. Smear due [TCI]. asd 126. Review Date 09/05/00

Mr J. Cameron & Ms C. Shepherd
Lloyds TSB new account
Opened 25/05/00
Transfer all from a/c 331690 84216940 and Co-operative Bank a/c 581290 61420072
All Standing Orders & DDs cancelled

The details that make or break the pattern: that's what we're looking for. We find it: on Cynthia's list at the chemist's. Very useful source, the prescription records. Great way to get to know your suspect. What makes them tick, often literally. Cynthia hasn't put in a new prescription for the pill this month.

What's more, James and Cynthia have just opened a joint bank account at Lloyds TSB. Cynthia has transferred her cash over – some savings but not massive. Take a second look at the DDs. No donation to Rape Crisis, no Women Against Violence. No Abortion Campaign. Smart girl, Prada girl. She knew what a giveaway these would be on her joint bank statement, bound to have raised a question before long. And the question would have led right to a fork in the road: yes or no, on or off. Truth or lie, that's easy; but it's in partial truth where most of us fall down, where most of us reside.

A good day's work for the Dogg. It reminds me of the great Sherlock Holmes. You may remember the famous case of the dog that didn't bark. Sherlock tracks down the killer because – no bark. The killer was known to the dog.

The Master Class: absence of information is as much of a clue as presence.

Lao Tze he say:

> Doors, windows, in a house,
> Are used for their emptiness;
> Thus we are helped by what is not,
> To use what is.

Withholding facts, that's a real nailer.

alanturing.net

THE TURING TEST

The interrogator is connected to one person and one machine via a terminal and therefore can't see his counterparts. His task is to find out which of the two candidates is the person and which is the machine, only by asking questions. If the machine can 'fool' the interrogator it is intelligent.

The test has been subject to different kinds of criticism and has been at the heart of many discussions in Artificial Intelligence philosophy and cognitive science for the past 50 years.

Finally an e-mail from Mr C.

> Just watch Robert for me. Forget the others.
> Sam Collier

29/05/00

<u>Anita File</u>

<u>UK news.local</u>

PEER'S DAUGHTER DIES OF DRUGS OVERDOSE

Anita Jettison, estranged daughter of Labour peer Lord Wilcox Barker, was found dead in her London flat yesterday. Ms Jettison, a production manager at leading advertising agency Saatchi & Saatchi, was discovered by police alone in her flat at 9.30 a.m. Police were alerted by Ms Jettison's cleaner. She is believed to have died from a drugs overdose. Investigations continue into the circumstances of her death [more].

I'm just about to go full on on Robert, when something happens none of us could have foreseen.

Anita is dead.

Anita, our little trustafarian. Found dead. Bland bodycopy in another press story no-one will remember for long.

The Dogg was interested in Anita, even got to like her. And she's gone. Now we have a death on our screens. A drugs overdose.

Just when you think you're mastering the process, getting a handle on the pattern, fate comes dancing round the corner – and he says: 'Bet you didn't expect to see me here.'

It's not James or Robert or Cynthia that's cracked. It's Anita.

01/06/00

Anita File

Campaign

THE BROADSHEET FOR THE ADVERTISING INDUSTRY

SAATCHIS' DOUBLE LIFE DRUGS VICTIM

The tragic death of Anita Jettison from a drugs overdose recently revealed a secret life. Ms Jettison, whose name was Anita Wilcox Barker before she changed it by deed poll, worked as a production assistant at Saatchis' Charlotte Street offices. Bert Rose, Production Director, said: 'This came as a complete shock to us all. Anita was a very private girl who kept herself to herself. She was extremely hard-working and conscientious. She had a bright future ahead of her and naturally we are all devastated by this news. We had no idea of her background.'

The reports of Anita's death. Very matter of fact in the national press. What interested the snoopers was her past. That's why no-one bothered to look into her present. They were all mesmerized by the money, and the way that the story fits into the proper cliché: poor little rich girl, you're a bewitched girl, bound to get your comeuppance.

The piece in *Campaign* was as guarded as you could get. The ad world also majored on her other life; jealous, no doubt. But notice there's no mention of our Roberto. No-one knew of their affair. No-one looked into their e-mail accounts like Dogg. Did the police bother with the electronic data dust? Doubt it. The guys from the Met didn't dig deeply enough.

A lesson to the sleuth. The facts which are always reported as facts – the newspaper truth – are not always facts. They are a story. That's what the journos call it and we happily comply with the game. So it's often what the press doesn't say that's really interesting to the investigator. Where are the gaps in the story; who was she with last night?

We die alone, but we don't necessarily plan to.

I'd overlooked the stuff on Anita's background. Want to check that there's nothing else I'm missing here.

I think again about the absence of information.

Japanese gardens; silence says more than sound. It isn't the columns of a Greek temple that hold the roof up, it's the spaces between them. It's the spaces between facts that shore up the story.

In my business it's called a hunch. How else do you describe a gap between data – a silence?

The week before Anita died, she disappeared. Took the week off work, we know that much. But there's not another single entry on any of her other data files for that week. No credit cards, no bank movements, no phone calls, nothing. She goes off the radar. Literally, because if she'd used her mobile, I could tell you not just who she called, but where she made the call from – to within ten yards. The uplink gives you away.

She must have taken a wodge of cash and just decided to head for the hills. Frustrating, for Dogg. The only real way to evade me is cash. If you don't withdraw, I know you're spending cash, but it's hard for me to find out on what.

More escape. How many times can this girl escape: from her name, her past, her present?

We don't know anything about that week. A simple mystery. Agatha Christie disappeared once; people could back then. She wouldn't get away with it now.

I take the unusual step. I don't believe in open searches. But on this occasion I have nothing to lose except my patience. I put in the names Anita and Anita Jettison and ask for a complete search on all files for that missing week. Only one reference: on a Missing Persons' column. A man on Skye writes:

> > Anita . . . 'Neat' . . . Remember: 'Skye is lovely and lonely.'
> Where did you go? I miss you. The island misses you. Call me.
> Write to me. E-mail me. I have the answer, Anita.

That sounds like our Anita all right. But would you go to Skye, on your own, if you were happy with your current life, or current lover?

www.deathclock.com

THE DEATH CLOCK

... Death Clock: the Internet's friendly reminder that life is slipping away ...

AIN'T NO WAY TO GO

A monthly cyberdigest of news and magazine articles about the curious ways people have died – some humorous, some horrific.

BORROWED TIME

A tastefully morbid page about death's literary aspects: in poetry, song lyrics and quotations.

THE CREMATION SOCIETY OF CAROLINAS

Basic, consumer-oriented facts about cremation and funerals to help plan for this difficult decision.

DEATH ARTICLES BY DR JONN MUMFORD

Death and Near-Death Experience site. An Eastern view of death, NDE, and a book review.

DEATH ON THE INTERNET

A collection of web pages on the Internet which embrace death in an informative or entertaining manner.

IS THERE LIFE AFTER DEATH?

Are people really dead after their life has come to an end – or is death a key which unlocks the door to some mystical afterlife? There is one [God] who knows the answer to all of these mysteries.

FOREVERLAND

Providing support for the loss of loved ones and promoting cultural relativity.

ROTTEN.COM

An archive of disturbing illustration.

No more dancing for Anita. Keep the fire burning in your eyes, girl. But for the Dogg, the file is closing. The data drying up, like the sinews in the body. Cry no more, ladies. Cry no more. That person who was once the life and soul of every party doesn't go out. Stays inside. Never to be seen again.

Death is a dodgy one for the Dogg. Can't get a handle on it. There are no facts, so you could say that there's nothing to know about death. It is an unknowable item. Sure, there's all sorts of paranormal propaganda, but none of that stacks up to information. Then there's religion. But that's about the triumph of belief. Nothing wrong in that, if that's how you want to lead your life. But no-one really says that life after death is a known fact. The strength – indeed the true test of faith – is to believe in something you can't prove. So how do I, Dogg, get the goods on Mr Death? No known abode. No credit cards. No life assurance policies. No nothing. The only way I can get to terms with it is through the emotions of people left behind.

Sadness. Grief. Loss. Absence. Darkness. This is the only stuff on death's file. If you can know anything about death, it is only through words like these. A silent scream. It pretends to meaning but has none. It is a nothing. Like Hector being dragged around the walls of Troy, his Achilles tendons used as ropes. But he is just dead.

If I were given the job of running down on Mr Death, all I could do is tell you about feelings. With something unknowable, feelings are the only facts. A nice conundrum for me.

22/06/00

Anita File

Daily Telegraph

DEATHS

Miss Anita Katherine Wilcox Barker. Much loved daughter, sadly missed. You will always be in our minds. Flowers to Golders Green Crematorium. Service at 11.30, 23rd June.

23/06/00

Robert File

Virgin Trains

First Class Return	£169.00		
Birmingham New Street			
Passenger	Mr R. Bolton		
Seat Reservation	23/06/00	11A	08.20
	23/06/00	11A	16.30

Robert Bolton
Electronic Diary
Saatchi & Saatchi

23/06   IKEA All day Birmingham=store check

Muswell Flowers
22/06/00

Bouquet	£30.00
Delivery Address	Golders Green Crematorium
	Re Anita Wilcox Barker

Paid	AMEX 3714 982416 3428 Exp. 02/01
Mr R. Bolton	Member since 1995

Anita's funeral is at Golders Green. Large crowd of friends and family. Anita was a popular girl. Full of fun, full of life. Snatched away so early.

So early.

At a little after 11.30 Anita was cremated. The last fact. Or maybe I should say the last is the crying. The family and friends inside the crematorium. Tears without relief. There is nothing good to be made of this. A coffin. A curtain. A brief reading from the Bible. The hymn. The end. People walk out into the sunshine. Walking out to nothing. Words exchanged without wanting to speak; the silent scream. For a father, a daughter lost. For friends, a friend gone. For love, no more.

Robert was not at the funeral; he was in Birmingham. He took the train and booked himself out all day at meetings with IKEA, his main account. That's OK; except that IKEA's head office is in Swindon. So this wasn't a client meeting full and proper. He was on a store visit. To get a feel for things. Non-essential visit. Could have been cancelled. Robert could have made it to the funeral. At least he sent some flowers. Credit card call – well, who pays for flowers for a funeral by cash these days?

Maybe he wrote to her family too. The Dogg's guess though is that he made no contact. Kept away.

Robert takes the 16.30 train back to London. No calls that evening. Incommunicado. Show us your colours, Robert.

Robert File

Amazon.co.uk
11/05/00

Hole, *Pretty on the Inside*	£11.99
Hole, *Live through this*	£11.99
Nirvana, *In Utero*	£7.99
Nirvana, *Never Mind*	£11.99
Jimi Hendrix, *Experience, Best Of*	£11.99
Janis Joplin, *Greatest Hits*	£7.99
The Doors, *Greatest Hits*	£7.99
Halperin and Wallace, *Who Killed Kurt Cobain?*	£11.99
Andrew Gracie, *Kurt Cobain* [*They Died Too Young*]	£11.50
Subtotal of Items	£95.42

Paid	Mcard
Mr R. Bolton	4323 7004 6110 9754 Exp. 09/00

That Internet tail I set on Robert is still running. But I ought to confess that I have missed stuff on Robert in the past. In the weeks before Anita's death, I didn't pick up enough on Robert's visits to some rather overt S and M sites. And he was making some unusual purchases – books and CDs – on the Net. Just shows, you have to recognize the pattern before you know what you're looking for.

Remember the file: Robert is a jazz buff. Member of Ronnie Scott's Club in Soho – and you probably don't just go there for the home cooking. Yet here is our young advertising man buying the likes of Nirvana, Hole and Hendrix. And that book: *Who Killed Kurt Cobain?*

Doing some research for an advertising pitch? Could be. But the Dogg believes that this is what's known as wavelength purchasing. You buy things to get on somebody else's wavelength. So you've got things in common to chat about. Drop the reference lightly into conversation. We've all done it; go through your music or book collection and don't tell me that lovers and partners haven't influenced a third of the choice. We borrow their interests, try them on for size, say that we fit.

That's what Robert was doing with kooky Kurt. Getting on Anita's wavelength.

Dogg did not spot the link in these purchases when they first came down on the screen. Did you? So many drug-related deaths. Spooky stuff, Dogg.

Anita File

Metropolitan Police Report

WORKING FOR A SAFER LONDON

File JettisonA 24355 8890
Report by DC Edwards No. 44134
Body discovered 27/05/00

I was called to attend a property at 24b Waltham Street, Chelsea, London SW3 7TH. I endeavoured to establish whether there was any person inside the property. However there was no reply. With the help of the housekeeper to the property, who held the keys, I then gained access through the front door. The lights inside the property were still on. I searched the downstairs areas. I was unable to find any person in these areas. I then proceeded to check the upstairs areas. I discovered the partly clothed body of a young female. White. Aged mid twenties to early thirties. I endeavoured to awaken the young female, but it was clear to me that the person was no longer alive. I called for medical support and waited at the scene until this arrived. The attending medical support team pronounced the young female dead at the scene.

Coroner's Report

MS ANITA JETTISON

Death from drugs overdose 26/05/00. Estimated time of death: 20.00–22.00 hrs on 26/05/00
Coroner's officers interviewed:

> Ms Sagradio Gonzalez [housekeeper]
> David Thoms [employer, Saatchi & Saatchi]
> Robert Bolton [colleague, Saatchi & Saatchi]
> Lynn Jacobs [friend]
> Lord Wilcox Barker [father]
> [Tapes filed]

Toxicology report 15/06/00: Dr Anthony Scholes: death by drugs overdose. Diamorphine. Bruises at wrists and ankles.
Coroner's verdict: death by drugs overdose. Accidental death.

www.kurtcobain.com

'I fake it so real I'm beyond fake'
Live Through This. Doll Parts. Courtney Love

Anita's file gives a final twitch. The guys at the Met did dig after all – brought Robert in for questioning. No doubt they accessed Anita's phone account to find out her most frequently called friends and had them in. Mutual regret over a tragic death. What a shocking waste of a young life. Another case for the drugs file.

The interview with Robert lasted an hour so they must have found something to talk about. But that's as far as it went. The autopsy confirms she died as a result of an overdose of cocaine. One small marginal comment: Anita had bruises to her wrists and ankles. Almost as though she had been tied up.

Still, no charges. Case closed. Verdict: Suicide. Sweet dreams, Anita.

Why no follow-up? Someone intervened, the Dogg can feel the sleeve of influence brush against the case. Wilcox Barker, eminent lawyer and Labour peer. Friend of the Lord Chancellor. Known to the Royal Family. Sandringham guest. 'No need to go poking around; Anita was always a wild one. It was just a tragic accident.'

The family didn't want any more investigations. And all justice begins with the notion of family. Because that's where the happiness started and where the sadness comes home. There is always a particular, liquid silence in the family house where mourners lie. Upstairs, in bed. In the middle of the afternoon. Eyes wide open.

No need to get Robert in again. His story stacks up. Yes, they were close friends, lovers even, but he never expected Anita would do anything like this. Oh really, Robert? I wonder what kooky Kurt would have to say about that.

Or Courtney Love: 'I fake it so real, I'm beyond fake.' Now there's a line that makes the hairs on the back of my neck prickle. I know what it is to fake beyond fake. I have seen people lie so much they believe their own lies. They cease to operate in the world of facts, the tangible data world of here and now.

Robert File

Threshers Wine Merchants
38 Waltham Street
Chelsea
London SW3 7TQ
26/05/00

1 Courvoisier VSOP	£14.99
Paid	AMEX
Mr R. Bolton	3714 982416 3428 Exp. 02/01
	Member since 1995
	Auth. 21.36

Anita disappears. Comes back to London. A few days later she's silent for ever. Suicide. The final escape: cocaine. Leaves with bruises to her wrists and ankles.

But I'm uneasy about this. Doesn't feel like Anita's pattern.

Besides, there's one small piece of information the Dogg would like to share with you. It's about Robert. Nobody in the investigation sought to blame him; his name wasn't mentioned in the press. The police interviewed him and let him go. No further questions. They would have done the usual checks. Looked at his telephone account for instance, so they would have known that the two were in touch and worked together.

But they wouldn't have checked out all the data. They wouldn't have known that Robert bought a bottle of Courvoisier at the booze store around the corner from Anita's flat at 9.36 that evening.

The coroner's report suggested that Anita died between 8 and 10 p.m.

I reckon Robert had to have been there. Not certain, but a reasonable deduction.

What we don't know, maybe, is whether Anita was dead when he left. Buying a bottle of brandy could take us either way. He went out to get a drink, got back and she was dead. Panicked, ran, covered up. Or he left knowing what had happened and the brandy was to help him forget. Death by overdose is never clean, never precise. Fatal mistake, suicide or assisted death. It could have been all or any of them.

Robert File

robbo@saatchi-saatchi.com
Last three website visits >>>
1. www.javajunkie.com
2. www.suicide.com
3. www.whybother.com

CLICK HERE

For photos of my friends who have died as a result of their powerlessness to addiction or consequences related to that disease. God Bless their souls and all I remember are good things about them – that no addict seeking recovery need ever die without finding a new way to live.

Robert's still roaming. His Net visits are erratic. He's trying to come to terms with things, needs to know why. Why did he help her? He knew what he was doing but didn't know; the body carrying out instructions from a mind that ceased to understand. Like sleepwalking into doors, you feel but don't.

And all the time Roberto's saying to himself: 'I just want to know what it feels like. To see someone slip away. She wants to go. I can help her. I can be there. I can be a voyeur and I'll be the only one who ever knows.'

Oh quiet, the Dogg. Prevent the Dogg from barking with a juicy bone.

SUICIDE LOSS FAQS

What is a suicide survivor? A suicide survivor has lost someone they loved or cared for deeply.

What help do suicide survivors need? One does not 'get over' a suicide. The effects may stabilize, but the loss is forever. Personal values and beliefs are shattered.

Robert File

www.bereavement.com

Visitor 234,386: robbo@saatchi-saatchi.com

Access: How We Die by Alexander Fletcher

Whatever happens in drug-related deaths, one thing we can be sure of. The testimony of those present is always deeply flawed. The combination of emotional intensity and physical extremity produces an hallucinogenic experience which is further distorted either consciously or unconsciously in the process of recollection.

ENGLAND AND WALES DRUGS-RELATED DEATHS 1997

Cause of Death	Instances
Heroin	255
Morphine	255
Heroin/morphine combined	455
Cocaine	38
Paracetamol compounds	561

It is Dogg's opinion that not even Robert really knows what went on that evening. If he tried to tell us what happened, the internal and external stories would get so mixed it would only be an impression. All sorts of internal stuff would cloud the facts. Sometimes the internals are so strong they cut out the facts, the breaker switch gets flicked through too much emotion, such that only the sensations remain true.

Anita can't tell us. Not even the Dogg can track her down now. So we will not know. And if we *could* know, what would it change? Would we be any the wiser? Naturally I don't like having unsolved situations. The Dogg goes truffling after truths. Unfortunate burden, the desire to know. Makes us human and unhappy. Creates cities and empires, discovers the anatomy of air, drives us to new worlds; yet ushers in the note of sadness. We cannot choose to stop knowing.

But this particular situation of uncertainty does not lead me to create the facts, or accept the truth of the internal story. In this case we shall not know. Nobody will know. Though the deep desire within us is to know, to have an explanation, to know who killed Monroe, or how exactly Princess Diana died, we shall not. Facts have occurred which never become facts. They remain hearsay, history, because the participants are dead. The Dogg suspects that many things are like this, a jumble of half-remembered voices, sensations in the night, between sleep and dream. Yet still taken as facts. Do not trust such information. Play with it, muse upon it, jumble it if you like. But stick to the facts. And accept the limits of knowing.

Robert File

Robert Bolton
Bank Account   First Direct
791290   68335710

Credit Zone   £5,000.00

Date	Item	Amount
27/05	Cash	£200.00
30/05	Cash	£300.00
02/06	Cash	£200.00
04/06	Cash	£200.00
07/06	Cash	£200.00
09/06	Cash	£300.00

Stringfellow's
The world's most famous nightclub!
05/06/00

            £248.00
Paid   AMEX
Mr R. Bolton   3714 982416 3428   Exp. 02/01
                 Member since 1995
                 Auth. 23.56

Whatever went on, Robert is dragging it with him. The Dogg detects the whiff of panic. The cash has started to flow again, £1400 in three weeks. Maybe even more telling, he now recognizes that he's out of control. Contacts Drugs Anonymous. Long call. He also makes two calls to his mother. More long chats. And as we've noticed before, Robert isn't exactly your average Mummy's boy. In fact, the last time he called her was when he moved out of James and Cynthia's flat and into his own place.

The excesses are showing elsewhere. A night out on the town capped with a visit to Stringfellow's and young girls dancing around the chrome poles. What is it about those poles that gets the punters going? Are they just phallic? That seems a bit obvious. Women find it all as much of a turn-on as men. I guess it's simply the idea of availability and control; those girls wrap and caress the pole but they can't get free. Bonded to it. And enjoying the bondage. Robert has dinner and champagne while the girls wriggle. In twisted minds.

www.datadetective.com

RCE INFORMATION SERVICES – FIND PEOPLE, COLLECT MONEY, JUDGEMENT, CATCH DEADBEATS

Try our new find anyone special! $49.95

www.datadetective.com

DATA DETECTIVE TECHNOLOGY – TURNING DATA INTO INFORMATION

www.globalcurrence.com/train_datadet.html

DATA DETECTIVE TECHNOLOGY TRAINING GLOBAL CURRENCE

Currence has created Data Detective, a one-day technology training . . . exclusively for law enforcement. Data Detective is comprised of . . .

www.sherlockat.com

SHERLOCK@ – THE INTERNET CONSULTING DETECTIVE: TIPS FOR SEARCHING

Learn how to use the Internet from the world's greatest detective, with informative articles.

www.profitbooks.com/detective/detective

THE CYBER-DETECTIVE TOOLKIT

Find Out Anything About Anyone Using The . . .

Reading about a Data Detective Convention. In Los Angeles. Imagine, nobody there, but everyone listening in!

Hell, there's lots of competition out there. Data detectives who will run down any fact you'll ever want to know, or any person you'll ever want to find. I'm maybe no better than them. But at least this case is new territory. And that gives me a head start. I'm beyond facts and into the now. I'm making the cross-over between dimensions; between observing and acting; between then and now.

Time to get back to Mr C.

I have some live facts to report. Facts which Mr C could get nowhere else but from me. Not from the police, or the press, or any other source. The Dogg alone knows:

> You asked for the tail on Robert. It takes us to a flat in Chelsea. A dead girl. Anita. Officially reported as a suicide in the press. But there's more to it than that. The facts I have suggest that Robert was there that night. Unclear as to whether he was actually in the house at the time of Anita's death, but I have a hunch he was. Also, one thing that doesn't fit in. Anita had fresh abrasions to her wrists and ankles. Could be she was tied up. Drugs and bondage. The big high. Since Anita's death Robert has been behaving erratically. I suggest that we keep the tail going and see where it will lead us. This will cost more.

yours, Dogg

25/06/00 09.35

<u>DOGG File</u>

81 Bryanston Road

Case closed.

Files running. Alert on active data.

Payment requested.

The reply from Mr C.

> Dogg.
> I do not want to know any more.
> You're making too many assumptions about people.
> Please send final invoice.
> Sam Collier

I'm off the job. Mr C has blown the whistle.

So all these weeks have been for nothing. For no obvious end. When you work for money, you stop when the money runs out.

Strange, that. Because the data is still running out there. Still adding to the files. The present keeps being topped up. The past is always present, because nothing is ever deleted. And the present is always future because there's no end to it, the file stays open, the data adds with each day.

At what point can you say this is 'now'? As soon as you've said it you're into the next. The now is eternal. That's what data means.

<u>**Cynthia File**</u>

MORI Newsletter

JULY 2000

'How Much Should We Know About Each Other?'

BY CYNTHIA SHEPHERD

In order to explore the issues raised by the Internet privacy debate I commissioned a so-called 'data detective' to investigate me. His name was Mr Dogg; thedogg@acdogg.co.uk. A pseudonym no doubt. He specializes in personal data [what he calls 'The Home Truths' package!] as well as tracking missing persons and collecting from runaway debtors. I posed as a 'Mr Collier', in order to see how far a stranger could go in learning about my public and private life. He accessed, by fair means and foul, an enormous mountain of data about me: from obvious details such as my phone numbers, bank and insurance accounts, to more intrusive data such as my private insurance records and my brushes with the law [two speeding fines]. What was really disturbing, however, was his ability to provide data on all my credit-card purchases. What's more, in response to my urgings, his 'research report' [sic] contained some pretty terrifying psychological interpretations of me. He could track my phone calls and log their frequency and length. He could also go back in time, for instance he found a record of a riding accident I had when I was a teenager . . . !

What are we to do about this potential for a society of voyeurs? The search made two things clear to me. First, these 'detectives' [hackers to you and me] have no sense of responsibility, no moral dimension to speak of. Second, corporate firewalls should be much more effective. So how do we frame the debate on the implications for research? Clearly, the notion of ownership is central. We must understand that we all own our own data. Everyone has, and needs, secrets, things which we choose to keep private. Invasion of our privacy should be seen as a crime – stealing what belongs to us, our data. We should be able to decide how much we want others to know.

In quality research projects this privacy is respected and guaranteed. Data is given up willingly [and in some instances for money], participants have a full knowledge that it will be used publicly [e.g. I share my views with a focus group] or that it will be protected. That is why the small print is there on the forms we fill out – to reassure us all on security and privacy. In conclusion I believe that responsible research should set limits on what we know directly about any one individual and on our ability to link up all the knowledge we gather.

Maybe Cynthia thinks I wouldn't pick up a piece like this. She under-estimates me. She thinks the file closes when the job stops. It doesn't. It's just that the customer doesn't get any more information.

I took Cynthia as someone who tells the truth. Remember her rape case; it was because she was honest that she didn't succeed. Now she's hiding things. She assumed another identity, lived a parallel electronic life. That's fine. Unlike her, but I can see why she did it – for pro-fessional purposes. To get me to show how good I was. Show me off in public and then deride what I do.

But there's a phrase in her report that's darker than the rest: *I hired a so-called 'data detective' to investigate me.* Forget the 'so-called' insult, the little word that sticks in my gullet is 'me'. Like Muhammad Ali says, Cynth, 'Me We'. I didn't just investigate you, Cynthia. You asked me to run down Robert – and James too. Even Anita. Why didn't you mention that in your so-called article? And why did you keep asking me to stick on Robert, then cave in just when I had given you the real facts about what went on with Anita that night?

You've got your secrets which you don't want people to know. But there's more to it than that. You're hiding things from me. You wanted to find out about Robert and James. You wanted to know everything: *Can't you do any better than that, Dogg?* There's a double motive going on here. You used me as a fall-guy for your article. But you actually wanted the facts on James and Robert too, didn't you, Cynthia?

Why did you stop me, Cynthia? Did I tell you something you didn't want to know?

Oh, and by the way, Cynth. Thanks for giving out my name in the article. Great publicity. Now I'll have every geek in the universe on my line.

04/07/00 09.34

DOGG File

81 Bryanston Road.

Files running.

Cynthia File

Burberrys
18/22 Haymarket
London SW1
03/06/00

Asst No. 306
12 Lds Rainwear   £295.00
SKU 4590001518719

Paid   VISA
Ms C. Shepherd   4550 9698 1291 7461   Exp. 03/01
Auth. 12.56

I reckon Cynthia got suspicious of something and wanted to get the lowdown. Hiding behind her article was a way to draw me out and to cover her real need to know.

Now she wants to ignore the data. She wants to unknow. But she can't unknow. Nor can I.

Robert was there the night of Anita's death. I can't prove it beyond doubt, but equally why would he have been just around the corner from Anita's pad and not called in? The balance of probability points to his finger on her doorbell. Walking in. Before or after her death?

Before. I'd bet my house on it, if I had one.

thedogg@acdogg.co.uk
File log: mail sorted by private client: name

Messages:

Shirley Dawson
Dogg I read about you in MORI Newsletter. I need to track down my daughter. She went missing 3 weeks ago. She has a credit card with her. Can you help? Please. We're running out of ideas.

Adrian Lovelace
I am trying to trace a debtor. He owes my company £34,000.00 and seems to have disappeared from the face of the earth. Will reward you handsomely for your help. Please call at number below for further information.

Nelson Deals
Dogg, you sound like a wise guy. Do you work for yourself or are you part of an outfit? I'd like to find out more about your work. I could help you.

Graham Sargent
Dear Mr Dogg, I am in the middle of a very messy divorce and suspect my wife of siphoning large sums from her account to banks abroad. Is this the sort of work you might be able to help out with?

Robert Bolton
I read an article in this month's MORI Newsletter about your services. I would be very interested in buying any files or information on Ms Cynthia Shepherd, Garden Flat, 81 Bryanston Road, London NW6. Would you please advise me as to whether you can supply these files and what they would cost.

Christina Shore
My sister has been missing now for 3 years. Just walked out of the house one day and never returned. The police have long since stopped looking for her, but we never give up hope. My family would do anything to know where she is and if she is safe. Do you handle cases of this nature? We desperately need your help.

At least Cynthia's article has done some good for me and my pro-fession. Proves that there's no such thing as bad PR.

This morning I get six new e-mails. New clients. From divorcees wanting to get the gen on their ex-husbands, to parents wanting help with runaway teenagers. Some of them are really heartbreaking. See me as their last resort, when perhaps I should have been the first. The first name on their address file. Favourite site.

But one sticks out. Robert wants Cynthia's file. First I was spooked – couldn't figure how Robert would have known about my work for Mr C. Then I checked the circulation of the *MORI Newsletter*. Goes to most of the big advertising agencies, including Saatchis'. And sure enough Robert Bolton is on the mailing list.

Robert reads the piece from Cynthia and wants to know more. You have to hand it to him. Chutzpah. Taking a big risk that I might let her know that someone else was after her private file. Just the thing that would scare old Cynthia; give her all that 'I told you so' material to hypervent on. Well, I sell my services to anyone. I have no choice. If I wasn't prepared to sell Robert the file on Cynthia, I'd be a mean little hypocrite, making all this big noise about freedom of information, but not prepared to take the tough decision when it comes along. I can't draw the line on what I will reveal and what I will keep secret. There is no censorship. Information is there, available to everyone, to glean, gather, mine. Do I want to give the file to Robert? No. Do I have to? Yes.

Robert wants the file. Now he can know everything about Cynthia.

06/07/00

From: thedogg@acdogg.co.uk
To: robbolton2@daemon.co.uk
Subject: Ms Cynthia Shepherd

Mr Bolton
Thank you for your enquiry about files on Ms Cynthia Shepherd of Garden Flat, 81 Bryanston Road, London NW6. I am sending you her complete file. The price is £750.00. I appreciate immediate payment. Should you need my services in any other way please contact me.

<u>Robert File</u>

acdogg
on-line payment
06/07/00

Fee	£750.00
Paid	AMEX
Mr R. Bolton	3714 982416 3428 Exp. 02/01
	Member since 1995

Mobile Tel. No. 07962 783 411

<u>Date</u>	<u>Time</u>	<u>Number</u>	<u>Duration</u>
07/07/00	15.10	07694 297 614	23.45 mins

I send the file to Robert.

And I'm going to watch every move he makes.

Next day, know what he does? He rings Cynthia. Mobile to mobile. A small detail, I know – but I'll bet he had her mobile phone number all along. But didn't use it until now. He's a fact gatherer who waits until the facts are ripe.

Robert File

Beacon Hotel
Birmingham
11/07/00

Room 217
1 Superior Double   £110.00

Extras
Dinner [x2]   £83.00
Minibar   £16.50
Total   £209.50

Checkout 9.15 a.m.

AMEX   Paid £209.50
Mr R. Bolton   3714 982416 3428   Exp. 02/01
                           Member since 1995

Robert takes the train to Birmingham. He stays at the Beacon Hotel. He takes a superior double room with queen-sized bed. His check-out bill confirms he paid for a dinner for two. They both had steak and one had chocolate ice cream. Washed down with two bottles of red wine.

James File

The World's Favourite Airline
BA Club World

10/07/00

BA 299 LHR ORD   dep. 11.15   arr. 14.10
Seat 4B

Return 12/07/00
BA 298 ORD LHR   dep. 17.45   arr. 07.30
Seat 15B

Mr James Cameron
BA Exec. Club No. 7388219 [Gold]

jamesc@aandersen.co.uk
12/07/00
Log on   11.13

James is away in the US. On a business trip. Flew out to Chicago, BA Business Class, two days ago. He leaves the following evening for Heathrow and goes straight into the office the next morning. Taxi booked by his office. Logs into e-mail at 11.13.

Cynthia File

Beacon Hotel
Birmingham
11/07/00

Room 419
1 Business Single   £74.00
Total   £74.00

Check out 8.32 a.m.

Paid   VISA
Ms C. Shepherd   4550 9698 1291 7461 Exp. 03/01

Cynthia is also travelling a lot, mostly for her job. Goes up to Birmingham.

Cynthia visits the Midlands fairly frequently – she was up in Leamington Spa a while back. So nothing out of the ordinary about this trip. Except she stays at the Beacon Hotel.

Typical business hotel. Soulless rooms pimped with tea and coffee makers. The empty space left by the Gideon Bible is filled by complimentary notepads. Not exactly halls of Blakean desire.

But that night there was desire. Robert and Cynthia. Together in the same hotel. He pays for dinner for two. She pays for no dinner.

Guess where she slept.

Robert File

Beacon Hotel
Birmingham
11/07/00

Restaurant Services

2 x Steak Frites	£36.00
2 x Château Beauséjour	£25.50
1 x Perrier	£3.00
1 x Choc Ice Cream	£6.50
2 x Coffee	£4.00
Service	£8.00
Total	£83.00

Transfer to room account 217
Mr R. Bolton [x2]

One anomaly in all this. Cynthia's a vegetarian. Yet the menu restaurant bill shows that Robert's partner that night had steak.

Interesting that, the vegetarian eating steak. Her mood, her hormones, or maybe the situation was just like having a chat with a girlfriend? She wanted to unload, talk to someone; still yearning to tell. That's of course supposing it was she who wanted to chat, who set the tenor of the evening. Could have been Robert. Could be that he just had to talk to someone about Anita and that night she died. Who on earth could he trust but the fragile Cynthia? You always seek other damaged vessels when you yourself are damaged. The strong, the unwrecked, will only tell you to be strong. But the damaged will allow you to indulge in your own tragedy. You rage against the madness, the unfairness, the impossibility of life. And they listen and agree; and the more mad, tragic, or impossible things sound in the swapping of tales, the better you feel. Briefly, the glow warms your hands.

All of this would be fine, if we didn't know that Robert has the file on Cynthia. He knows everything about her. Everything. More than James. That changes things, doesn't it? See what I told you. What information, when. That's the key to this business of mine. Because you know that Robert has bought Cynthia's file, it shapes what you think about what went on that night.

Cynthia. Lured. Stalked. You had the data yet chose to ignore it. But Robert's a predator. He wanted the information so he could get to you. Maybe that's not all that surprising. That's how lots of relationships get started: finding out what interests the other; finding common ground. The difference of course with my data is that it goes much deeper. It tells secrets. And secrets can be used by the unscrupulous.

INTRODUCTION TO PRINCIPLES OF MORALS AND LEGISLATION

BY JEREMY BENTHAM

OF MOTIVES

Motive refers necessarily to action. It is a pleasure, or pain, or other event, that prompts to action. Motive then, in one sense of the word, must be previous to such events. But for a man to be governed by any motive he must in every case look beyond that event which is called his action; he must look to the consequences of it: and it is only in this way that the idea of pleasure, of pain, or of any other event, can give birth to it.

People put too much emphasis on motive. They think it explains every-thing. Me, I usually don't worry about the 'why'. I look for the 'who'. 'Why' is a messy area. It messes up your brain. I recognize the power of motive. It's the unseen force that drives the act. The feelings that force you forward. But because it's unseen, it's always a guess. Shooting theories into the dark. I say you can't rely on motive, because you can't prove it until afterwards. It's the easy, lazy way to investigate. I know the emotions are there, I can feel the passions beneath the facts. But I won't let myself be led by them. The only way to work is to stick to the truth. Detached. Objective.

Cynthia wanted to find out about Robert and James as part of her little experiment. Could be, as I've said, she even used the article as a cover for checking them out. Robert deliberately gets hold of the file on Cynthia. So there's not too much difference there. Their motives were roughly the same. But Cynthia ultimately doesn't want to know. She wants to rely on her instincts. She doesn't use the data.

Robert not only wants to know, he puts the data to work. And, inter-esting, he hasn't come back for more. He wanted the secrets on Cynthia, but not to track her.

Some people will use facts for good and some for bad; some will use them for selfish reasons and others just for fun. You can't lock up information just because of motive.

Interflora
18/07/00

1 bouquet   £30.00
Ms C. Shepherd
Paid   VISA
                                    4550 9698 1291   Exp. 03/01
Delivery address   Mr J. Cameron
                                    Arthur Andersen
                                    1 Surrey Street
                                    London WC2R 2PF

From Cynthia Shepherd

Message   *With love from C*

I could get into their lives: Cynthia, Robert and James.

If I really want to get into someone's life all I have to do is assume their identity. As the Dogg has told you, every call you make, every payment slip you sign leaves a data trail. But is it your trail, or did someone steal your identity for a while? Anyone who's had their credit card stolen will know the feeling. It's not just money going out of your account that hurts, someone out there is using the convenience of electronic communications to become you. That's what happens when you create a virtual world of @. You can move between people, take on their personalities, indulge in the ultimate tourism – 'identity tourism'.

I don't have to stoop to actually stealing cards to travel to new people. No need to. If I need to swap identities, become the other person electronically, I have everything I need for the matchless disguise. I know their habits, their bank accounts, their whole data bank even. The trick is to assume their personality; move and communicate through their data files.

The Dogg can start paying for things on their credit cards. Leaving traces on their tracks. Sending messages from their e-mail. Change entries on their phone accounts. I can do this to anyone. I could do it to James or Robert or Cynthia. The Dogg could be James or Robert or Cynthia.

Let me show the world that there is a bridge between dimensions. I shall be Cynthia and James shall feel my touch in the night, as though it were Cynthia's.

The Dogg buys James some flowers using Cynthia's credit card. The flowers are sent to his office. The card is signed *With love from C.*

When the flowers arrive at James's office, I am Cynthia. I can be anyone, to anyone. The Dogg can disappear into you.

I could send a message to the police or Robert, Cynthia or James – and they'd never know who sent it.

18/07/00

<u>**Cynthia File**</u>

e-mail log: cynths@mori.org

<u>Time</u>	<u>From</u>	<u>Subject</u>
09.14	sdjames@able.co.nl	'Shell Review'
11.23	ghadams@skb.com	'Last Invoice'
12.56	jamesc@aandersen.co.uk	'Flowers'

I can't resist breaking my own rule. I check out Cynth's e-mail list, just to see whether the plan works. Sure enough, old James sends her a note, subject: Flowers. 'And it was so darling of you to remember!' he says. Remember! Cynth thinks: 'Christ, remember what?' Cynthia has forgotten whatever it was. She didn't send him flowers, but is she going to quiz him about it? The Dogg thinks not.

So when Cynthia gives James a kiss tonight, she will really be kissing Dogg. Gets you thinking. If one wanted to commit the perfect crime, you'd do it electronically. If you really wanted to kill someone you wouldn't use a gun or knife, you'd use a cursor. You'd kill and leave the trail right back to yourself, only you wouldn't be 'yourself'. Because you'd have planted the information onto that identity. You would have assumed another's identity to carry out the perfect crime. A crime undetected, undetectable. Is that why the world fears the hacker? Is it because there is no end to what his skills can achieve, no end to the loss of identity that comes with @? Electronic media erode the identity; you can lose yourself in dataland. The prophecy rings true: 'no man is an island, entire of itself'.

THE DECEPTION TOOLKIT HOME PAGE AND MAILING LIST

OUR MISSION

Our mission is to discuss issues surrounding deception and the deception toolkit from the definition of what it is and how to do it and everywhere between.

The basic idea is not new. We use deception to counter attacks. In the case of DTK, the deception is intended to make it appear to attackers as if the system running DTK has a large number of widely known vulnerabilities. DTK's deception is programmable, but it is typically limited to producing output in response to attacker input in such a way as to simulate the behaviour of a system which is vulnerable to the attacker's method. This has a few interesting side effects . . .

Brave New Work

THE TANGLED WEB OF E-DECEPTION

In the old days, managers asked their secretaries to lie. Now they ask their technologies.

Attitudes Towards Sexual Relations 1998

	Always wrong	Mostly wrong	Sometimes wrong	Rarely wrong	Not at all wrong	Other
A man and woman having sexual relations before marriage	8	8	12	10	58	5
A married person having sexual relations with someone other than their spouse	52	29	13	1	2	4
A boy and a girl having sexual relations aged under 16	56	24	11	3	3	3
Sexual relations between two adults of the same sex	39	12	11	8	23	8

Deception. What is the nature of deception? I have just deceived James. Cynthia has just deceived James.

I sent him flowers. She was with Robert. Very different crimes. But the act of deception is exactly the same. The curtain drawn across the window; the false trail left.

We use the same techniques to hide treachery or tryst.

I have deceived electronically; she physically. Will the techniques change with technology? It seems to me that lies will always be lies.

But more to the point, where do you draw the line between acts of deception? Was my little act any less unacceptable than Cynthia's? At what moment did Cynthia's meeting with Robert become deception? When they set it up [if they did – it could be a coincidence they were both there in the Beacon Hotel]? When they met for dinner [harmless enough; two friends having dinner together]? What if she had left his room at 11 p.m.? Would that have been all right? Or 12.30? At what point did the deception become unacceptable?

That's it. Because it's so difficult to draw the line, deception happens. Before you've realized it, one drink leads to a hangover. Human nature. That's why I say the only safe way to play these things is to keep to the files; you did or you didn't do it. But that's hard for humans.

Robert File

Robert Bolton
Expense Reporting
Corporate American Express Card 3714 982416 3428 Exp. 02/01

Date	Amount	Item	Cost Code
22/06	£83.69	Lunch	IKEA03
26/06	£30.00	Hospitality	S/S General
06/07	£750.00	Data for researching target audience lifestyle	IKEA03
11/07	£209.50	Travel (hotel)	IKEA03

Robert's expenses. They make interesting reading.

Cynthia File

Market Research Annual Conference
26/07/00–28/07/00

26/07/00: AFTERNOON SESSION: RESEARCH AND ETHICS

15.30   'Dangerous Data: How much should we know about each other?'
               Cynthia Shepherd, Mori Organization

Metropole Hotel
Brighton
26/07/00–28/07/00

Room 627
One Single   £90.00 [x2]
Phone

Time	Number	Duration
18.45	020 7604 3940	2.35 mins
18.53	020 7604 3940	2.69 mins
Total	£185.03	

Paid   VISA
Ms C. Shepherd   4550 9698 1291 7461   Exp. 03/01

Robert File

Robert Bolton
Saatchi & Saatchi Electronic Diary
26/07–28/07   MRS

Kings Hotel
Brighton
26/07/00–28/07/00
Room 116

One Deluxe Double Room	£125.00 [x2]
Minibar	£27.00
Films	£26.50 26/07 [*She Likes It*; *Batman Returns*; *R. Lolita*]
	£9.00 27/07 [*Swedish Holiday*]
Total	£312.50

Paid   AMEX
Mr R. Bolton   3714 982416 3428   Exp. 02/01
                   Member since 1995

Cynthia is attending a conference in Brighton. Giving another paper on Data and Privacy. Trying to make a name for herself. Calls the speech 'Dangerous Data: How much should we know about each other?' Nice title, Cynthia. Bet I come in for more derision. That's because she's scared of me. Because I represent her new nightmare: no censorship. Censorship has always been presented as the mean little guy in the corner. The silent type. Wears wrap-around specs. The one you have to fear most. The guy that rang the Nazis' bell; he was there at Auschwitz; he was there in Laos. He was whispering in George Orwell's ear: 'Evil will take your language and use it to tell lies. The same language you love, I will corrupt. The truth must not out. Clean the words of meaning. Censor them.' Poor George, he was so right he was wrong. Because he made it so real, so worrying, the world was on its guard. We could see who the bad guys were, we thought. And we fought against them, hard and tough. Freedom of speech. Free press. Open government.

But, Cynth, you're not afraid of censorship. Secretly. Way, way down, you think the battle's won [not that you'd ever admit it]. A little censorship doesn't harm. It stabilizes. Now I'm the bad guy, because I am Mr 'No Censorship'. Because neither you nor George ever saw me coming. Let everything be known. Information wants to be free. And you know what? That's real scary. The future is worrying because everything can be known. Everyone's secrets. The secrets of life itself. And, Cynth, you and everyone, the educated and the ignorant, don't know what to do about that.

Back to the action. While Cynth's doing all this talking, she stays with the other conference attendees at the Metropole Hotel. Robert also visits Brighton. Checks into the Kings Hotel. For the same two nights that Cynthia is in Brighton. Unrelated? What about the fact that Robert pays for a dinner for two? More conjecture? The Dogg leaves it to you. And Robert's hotel bill that night. Lots of movies – all through the night. Stayed awake. Active. And the movies make interesting viewing: *She Likes It, Batman Returns* and *Russian Lolita. Batman Returns* isn't the usual adult movie choice. Although the Dogg has to admit to the joyous presence in the movie of La Pfeiffer as Cat Woman. Those cartwheel flips! That leather suit! 'Miaow'!

08/08/00

James File

The World's Favourite Airline
BA Club World
BA 235 LHR JFK   dep. 08.50   arr. 11.30
Seat 15B

Mr James Cameron
BA Exec. Club No. 7388219 [Gold]

Robert File

Barbican
Silk Street
London EC2
09/08/00
2 x Tickets *Le Mépris*   £18.00

Paid   AMEX
Mr R. Bolton   3714 982416 3428   Exp. 02/01
                                 Member since 1995

Manna
4 Erskine Road
London NW3
09/08/00

Meal   £41.00
Paid   AMEX
Mr R. Bolton   3714 982416 3428   Exp. 02/01
                                 Member since 1995
                                 Auth. 23.35

Just over a week later. James is travelling again. Back to the States. New York. Imagine that.

Robert pays for two tickets to see *Le Mépris* with Bardot; part of the Jean-Luc Godard season at the Barbican. He has dinner with another at Manna. It's a vegetarian restaurant. Robert is not a vegetarian. So the person he has dinner with must be.

Robert is paying for someone.

James is away again.

Robert is using that file I sent him. Getting on Cynth's wavelength. Taking her to art films. I bet the last time Robbo went to see subtitles was at university. On a Sunday night. And even then it wasn't his idea of fun; he was surfing the wavelength of another girl in blue jeans.

23/08/00

James File

The World's Favourite Airline
BA Club World
BA 1498 LHR Edinburgh   dep. 09.00
Seat 11A
James Cameron
BA Exec. Club No. 7388219 [Gold]

Caledonian Hotel   0131 223 4861
Edinburgh
Room 424
1 Executive Single   £138.00
James Cameron
Reserved 23/08–24/08

Tel. No. 020 7604 3940
81 Bryanston Road
London NW6 8KR

Time	Number	Duration
22.15	0131 223 4861	12.09 mins
22.30	07962 783 411	1.46 mins

Robert File

LOVERS' LIMOS
The Ultimate London Love Sexy Machines. Total Comfort. Total Discretion.
'Love your way over London'
23/08/00

23.30	£250.00
Paid	Mcard
Mr R. Bolton	4323 7004 6110 9754 Exp. 09/00

24/08/00	
Balance Refund	£125.00
Balance to	Mcard
	4323 7004 6110 9754 Exp. 09/00
	Auth. 03.45

Two weeks later. James is on business in Edinburgh on the Wednesday night.

Robert books a limo.

I check them out. Called 'Love Wagons'. Your own limo for the night. And I mean night.

Cynthia phones James at 10.15.

Robert puts a deposit on the limo journey at 11.30. He pays the final tab at 3.45 a.m.

Sex in the back of a limo. Not everyone's fantasy, but there's a market. Tour London while you're doing it. Gives a whole new meaning to Shaftesbury Avenue. And how else could you make love by the steps of St Paul's or passing No. 10?

Smoked windows, leather seats. Video on. A drinks cabinet. The fun is the uncertainty. Maybe the driver knows what's going on, maybe he doesn't. Maybe those windows aren't quite as opaque as you thought: the outline of shifting shadows greets the bag ladies of Piccadilly Circus.

SPIRITWEB: THE HEART'S CODE

Cynthia is ignoring the data. If I sent her another e-mail, warning her to lay off Robert, reminding her that Robert was there that night with Anita, she'd probably just reply: 'That's not what he says.' And she'd believe him and not me. After all, 'he knows her so well'.

Cynthia is one of those people who live by paradigms. She creates a fiction out of what she knows and what she wants the facts to be. There's a private code going on inside her head. It filters. It creates the reality she wants.

Most people write the book on life as part fact and part fiction. And Cynthia doesn't want her code broken.

That's what she's getting at in her little lectures: How much should we know about each other? It's fine to have the stats on people you never meet. That's what Cynthia does for a living, after all. But it's not fine to have the facts on people you know intimately. Not fine to have them on your husband or wife, your lover or your sister. Because these facts may not match with your internal version and it's too hard to change that picture. Too painful. You don't want to have to change the picture.

A new insight: not just what information, when; but what information, who. The 'who' matters. People still want to draw the line differently for different people. I say, this is the new Fall. You can't draw the line. The Tree of Knowledge is in your own back garden. Always. The file will be forever open. Is this heaven on earth or very hell?

Look deep, Dogg. Can you choose to unknow? Can you choose not to know? How far can trust, the great protector, take you? Can trust hold on, can trust hold out?

Who do you think you are, Dogg? God? You gave the stuff away on Cynthia and now look what's happened. People are deceiving, lying, being unfaithful and all because of that one file. The person who's in the dark is James. He loves. He trusts. And he's the one wearing the cuckold's horns tonight. It shouldn't happen. But it does.

www.hamlet.org/hamlet_essays

SOME ESSAYS ON HAMLET

The following are essays from a variety of sources. In cases where an author is contemporary and on-line, the name will be highlighted underneath the title. If you wish to submit an essay for consideration please review our guidelines.

'A Study of Rosencrantz and Guildenstern' by Lois Simpson
'Hamlet and Fortinbras' by Fayza Tanzeen Ahmed
'The Hamlet Paradigm' by John S. Mamoun
'Hamlet and his Problems' by T. S. Eliot [offsite, use 'Back' button to return here]
Two reprints courtesy of the Georgia Shakespeare Festival's production of Hamlet
'Dramaturg' by Amlin Gray
Excerpt from Peter Zadek's 'Hamlet' by Stefan Steinberg
'A Hamlet Interpretation' by F. C. Hunt
Reprinted, with permission, from Sir Francis Bacon's New Advancement of Learning
'Notes on Hamlet' by Samuel Johnson
'Hamlet: Weakness or Justice' by Benjamin Scott-Hopkins

The Sacred Wood: Hamlet and his Problems

BY T. S. ELIOT

Qua work of art, the work of art cannot be interpreted;
there is nothing to interpret . . .

www.colby.edu/personal/leosborn/hamletpage

19TH CENTURY HAMLET TEXT ILLUSTRATION

For example, I could also use Hamlet's gesture to the left to illustrate how the ghost's presence disrupts Hamlet's language literally in this scene . . .

Are our lovers feeling guilty about deceiving James? I think they'd have to admit at least to feeling uneasy.

If we asked them, what excuses would they give? That they never meant it to happen or that from the first time they clapped eyes on one another it was inevitable?

Whatever they said, it wouldn't move things on. We can't really get to know. Yet there are whole swathes of literature that deal in just this ridiculous quest: peeling off the layers of the subjective onion. Slowly revealing the psychology at work. Like in *Peer Gynt*. Or like *Hamlet*. An endless meandering of the soul. Soliloquy upon soliloquy. And nothing happens. The fascination of the play for generations is founded on a hoax. People get all uptight about finding the meaning of *Hamlet*. But there is no meaning. We just get endless inner speak, a man explaining how he feels. And, surprise, surprise, how he feels changes, is inconsistent, falters, wavers, shifts. It's the internal story run riot. Hamlet for all his words, words, words doesn't say a thing.

So what I say is: Thank God for the Sword Fight. Action at last!

And you know what, I think old William knew all this. He gets given this story about Amleth, Gerutha, Feng and Horwendil, told to turn it into a play and . . . there's no action. One measly little sword fight – hell, the Elizabethans were used to loads of them. Practically the whole cast getting nobbled on stage. Blood. Guts. Revenge. And what does Will have in *Hamlet*? What does he get to swing the crowd? One sword fight! 'Oh, it won't do,' he says. 'No. No. They'll be throwing rotten apples before the end of the first act. Merciless, they are. Ruthless. And next door they've got bear-baiting! What chance do I have!' Then he comes up with a brilliant wheeze: 'What if I just get this guy to talk about action and never do any? You know, just wander around on stage talking about his immortal soul, and how he might do it, and how he could do it, and if only the time was right he would do it.' Well, of course the crowd get mesmerized. Can't make head nor tail of it. Can't understand what's going on. Sounds as if something's going to happen any minute – but it never does. They're so confused that Will pulls it off. And Eng. Lit. was never the same again.

30/08/00

<u>Cynthia File</u>

Boots the Chemist Ltd
Hays Galleria
London SE1
30/08/00

1 x Egg and Cress Sandwich	£1.25
1 x Orange Juice	£1.05
1 x First Response	£8.99
1 x Cotton Buds	£1.67
Total	£12.96

Paid	VISA
Ms C. Shepherd	4550 9698 1291 7461 Exp. 03/01

Boots Advantage Card	492148986
Previous pts total	1380
Pts awarded	42
New pts total	1422

Want to have fun with your photos? Make good photos even better? Share them with Friends and Family all round the world? At Boots not only can we produce top quality photos, we can also capture your photos onto a CD or disc. Put the CD or disc into your PC and then the fun really begins! Taking the picture is just the start!

There is a painting by Seurat. *La Grande Jatte.* You know the one. Modernism's *fête champêtre.* 'I want to show the moderns moving about on friezes,' said Seurat. Modern men and women painted in the heroic and ordinary light of a sunny afternoon on the banks of the Seine. Bourgeois Paris in its finery. The picture seems to show leisure, small groups who seem to have something in common, yet don't. The man with the pipe and cap sits next to a woman with a bonnet. They are a few inches apart yet come from different worlds. Nobody knows each other. No eyes meet. No hands are held. Nobody talks. It's an idyllic afternoon yet no-one's enjoying themselves. The preposterous figure in the centre, the one who seems to wear a bandsman's helmet and plays a trumpet, is playing to no-one. Is the little girl skipping, or running away? A scene of people together in their isolation.

You can see the same picture in parks and green spaces across the cities of the world. Lunchtime masterpieces, when office workers emerge from behind their desks and, for a brief hour, remember the feel of sunshine and grass. With sandwiches made of coronation chicken, ham and wholegrain mustard, prawns in mayonnaise. A demi-Eden, for people who come alive at the lunch hour, and never say a word.

This lunchtime Cynthia visits Boots the Chemist. The place where things get sorted. Everyone's High Street fix. Cynthia buys a pregnancy testing kit.

James and Cynthia are at home that night. Several telephone calls out. A takeaway in.

RESULTS FOR EDEN, GARDEN OF

. . . in the BIBLE, the first home of humans. God established the garden, with its trees of knowledge and life as a dwelling place for ADAM and EVE . . .

Eden. That's where it all started. Where A and E gained their sense of privacy. Without knowledge of self, there can be no sense of privacy. I mean, animals don't ask us to respect their privacy. But knowledge of self leads to knowledge of others. And so they covered their 'private parts' with fig leaves.

Thinking more about Cynthia and Robert. And her need for privacy. In privacy lies deception. In fact, that's the cost of privacy. Privacy requires all of us to conceal not just facts about ourselves, but actions. Cynthia calls it her private life. Of course she'd also say that privacy protects. We have a right to privacy, as sacred as any enshrined in any universal Charter of Human Rights. She'd also say that there's a difference between private data, and data which is in the public interest and therefore should be available to all.

She wants it both ways. She wants protection *for* herself. But she also wants protection *from* others.

For and from. Two little prepositions that construct most people's view of the world. But I guess I say that for and from are the same thing. There's a cross-over between public data to private data; the boundaries have come down. This is the borderless world.

It isn't privacy that protects, Cynthia. It's trust that protects. It's love that protects. So, playing devil's advocate, here's a new interpretation of the Fall: we have gone beyond knowledge, because everyone has it. This is the new age of emotions. Emotions save us from rational thought. The brain is just a tool. Emotions will get us through. What matters is the training of the heart, not to deceive, but to believe.

Are you going soft, Dogg? It's getting to you, isn't it? Want to crack. Want to cross the line. Want to send a warning message to James. Want to send James the file on Robert. The up-to-date file, that is. That might be the most obvious decent thing to do, because you're involved with these characters now. You're part of their fate. But crossing the line is not the answer. You can't interfere, Dogg. You're just the channel to information. They have to make up their own lives.

31/08/00

Cynthia File

**Boots the Chemist Ltd
Hays Galleria
London SE1
31/08/00**

1 x Orange Juice	£1.05
1 x Tuna	£1.65
1 x Folic Acid	£3.60
Total	£6.30

Paid	VISA
Ms C. Shepherd	4550 9698 1291 7461 Exp. 03/01

Boots Advantage Card	492148986
Previous pts total	1422
Pts awarded	20
New pts total	1442

192.com
020 7515 2111   Abortion Advice Line

Mobile Tel. No.
07694 297 614

Time	Number	Duration
15.34	020 7515 2111	23.45 mins

Another lunchtime. And Cynthia walks back into Boots. Back to the sandwich section and then off to health supplements.

Now, the Dogg is no expert on pregnancy, but when a woman buys folic acid it normally means she's pregnant.

But when the same woman rings the Abortion Advice Line, it definitely means she's pregnant. In fact, that's the only definite thing going round Cynthia's mind. The rest of it is scrambled eggs – as it were. Conflicting messages: buying folic acid says she wants to keep it; calling the Abortion Advice Line says she doesn't. No idea what to do next. Does she keep the child or not?

01/09/00

<u>Cynthia File</u>

MediSearch . . . accessing files Dr Gavin Richardson . . .
patient: Ms C. Shepherd
Dr Gavin Richardson
01/09/00

Pregnant 6/40. Unplanned but happy. Para 0+o. LMP 17/07 certain. EDD 30/04/01. Regular cycle 5/28. No PV bleeding. Taking folic acid, non-smoker. PHM – not signif – Rubella immune. C/S Nov 99 negative. FH nil relevant. O/E BP 110/70. Urinalysis – no protein no sugar. Discussed antenatal care, diet, alcohol, exercise.

<u>Plan</u>
Refer midwife for booking appt, dating scan – nuchal fold scan. Practice advice sheet leaflet given. Follow up – see GP after booking appt.

Tel. No. 020 7604 3940
81 Bryanston Road
London NW6 8KR

<u>Time</u>	<u>Number</u>	<u>Duration</u>
21.45	01844 278881	12.34 mins

192.com
01844 278881   Manoir Aux Quat' Saisons, Great Milton

Manoir Aux Quat' Saisons
Great Milton
Oxon
03/09/00

1 De Luxe Suite	£650.00
2 Menu Gourmand @ £78.00	£156.00
1 Champagne	£44.00
Total	£850.00

Paid	Lloyds Mcard
Mr J. Cameron	4775 9180 2227 4176 Exp. 12/00
	Auth 11.34

She's slept on it and made up her mind. She's going to have the baby all right. And everything's fine. She's a picture of health. Damn vegetarians.

She tells James about the baby that evening. Why? Well, why else does he ring a swanky place like the Manoir Aux Quat' Saisons at nine o'clock on a Friday and book the best suite in the place?

They're off celebrating.

LETTERBOX

TURN IDEAS INTO SCREENPLAYS WITH LETTERBOX!

LetterBox is an innovative screenplay and scriptwriting software tool which grants aspiring screenwriters the power to create professional scripts and screenplays without professional scriptwriting knowledge

04/09/00

James File

jamesc@aandersen.co.uk
Lotus Notes

04/09 13.00   Lunch Robert

Robert and James meet for lunch at Number One Aldwych. It's the first time that they've met in weeks, could be months. Not since Robert moved out. Nice place for a meal. I picture it going something like this:

Scene 42: Interior Restaurant

Close-up on James's face: studying the menu. He puts it down and looks at Robert, who is still apparently engrossed in his menu.

JAMES: So. How's it going?

ROBERT: Fine, thanks, fine.

JAMES: The flat OK?

Robert now looking at James.

ROBERT: Yeah, it's good. Not too far from the tube and having the place to myself has been good for me. Given me space.

JAMES: Didn't know you needed space, Robbo – you've always been a bit of a cuddly-boy really. Chasing other people's orange juice round the fridge. Remember that flat we had in Bristol? Who was it that threw the orange juice at you? . . . Gail, was it?

ROBERT: No, Suzanne – Gail was your little fling.

JAMES: Gail. The human octopus. The girl with kaleidoscope eyes. Anyway, happy times . . . So you want to know the really good news?

ROBERT: God. Can I stand good news?

JAMES: Cynthia's pregnant.

Cut to Robert's face: eyes widen, nothing more.

JAMES: Fantastic, isn't it? The Cameron genes are to be continued. Glad tidings for mankind . . .

05/09/00

Robert File

Mobile Tel. No. 07962 783 411

Time	Number	Duration
10.05	020 7630 7096	6.40 mins
11.45	020 7630 7096	10.54 mins
14.40	07694 297 614	9.51 mins

Perhaps just my imagination; Robert and James could have just gossiped about work and life and the bum rap that life is. But old friends meeting for the first time in months: I bet they talked about the news. It would have been too important to James not to.

And I think James must have said something juicy to Robert because the next day he calls him at the office twice. Rare thing. Then he calls Cynthia straight after.

12/09/00 21.35

<u>Cynthia File</u>

Odeon Leicester Square
12/09/00

2 x Tickets *Madame Bovary*   £13.00

Paid   VISA
Ms C. Shepherd   4550 9698 1291 7461   Exp.03/01
                                 Auth. 18.56

Selfridges Beauty Hall
12/09/00

1 x Allure Eau de Parfum 50 ml £48.00

Paid   VISA
Ms C. Shepherd   4550 9698 1291 7461   Exp. 03/01
                                 Auth. 13.07

Cynthia's been to the movies again, this time to see *Madame Bovary*. Probably with a girlfriend; ideal girls-evening fare. But the choice of movie is interesting. Cynthia wishing to compare her experiences with Madame Bovary? Checking out the wild carriage ride sequence with her own mad driving? Not so far-fetched, Dogg, people check themselves out against fiction all the time.

Remember small behavioural signals, that's what we're looking for. Slight flecks that change the pattern. Choice of movie conveys mood; choice of perfume – well, that goes deeper. James bought Cynthia Chanel No. 5. Presumably that's what she's been wearing over the past months. Now, during her lunch break earlier today she buys Allure; still Chanel but a very different scent. Younger, less classic, more come-and-get-me.

Could be several explanations for Cynthia's change. She could have fallen for the marketing; wanted to see herself differently. Wanted to *be* slightly different. She may have acted on a whim; got caught by a free tester, liked the scent and bought it on impulse. Or it could signal a change of man. Maybe there was no single reason, simply a subtle collection of influences. But right now it's a choice worth noting.

When Cynthia gets back that evening, she will smell slightly different to James.

13/09/00

<u>James File</u>

jamesc@aandersen.co.uk
Lotus Notes

Dr S. Faversham
182 Harley Street
London W1N 2AP

13/09 11.00–12.00   Appt. Dr Faversham [020 7229 9890]

Computacab
A. Andersen Account

<u>Name</u>	<u>Destination</u>	<u>Time</u>
J. Cameron	81 Bryanston Road	21.30

James is slaving away as usual. Hasn't even had a holiday this year; just one weekend away at the Manoir celebrating. Then I notice he blocks off an afternoon in his diary – when he's really busy. The note in the entry says Dr S. Faversham.

I check him out. Let's just say that if you've got a problem with your big toe, you don't go to Dr S. Faversham. This is about something much more specific and much more specifically male. Here we have Cynthia pregnant and James is off to a private health clinic. Doesn't compute.

The appointment is for an hour.

So James walks in, takes a seat and starts to talk. Not easy. But, he thinks, the doctor must have heard all this stuff before so there's no point beating about the bush. Tell it straight. He's left this doubt hanging over him for too long. The problem with the testes. Is he fertile? He wants to know.

Still doesn't compute though. His girlfriend is pregnant and he's checking out his fertility?

After the appointment with Dr S. Faversham, James takes a taxi back to the office.

He stays late at the office that night. Books a cab home at 9.30.

James File

File Cam2455: James Cameron

Dr S. Faversham
182 Harley Street
London W1N 2AP
13/09/00

In LT relationship. Concern over medical history. No major investigations. Sperm analysis.

Sample sent for test. Confidential. Client informed.

Inventory Notes

Shortfall

1 syringe/needle
2 packets swabs
1 pair rubber gloves
Assumed lost in transit

No. of patients seen Tues. 13/09/00 6
No. of cancelled appts 2
No. of bills unpaid after 30 days 12

Just another suspicion, but the Dogg checks out Dr Faversham's files. James did have a fertility test. The results don't show, but there is a note on the file 'Client informed'. Not clear whether that means the client has been informed that the test has been sent for analysis, or that the results are through. The Dogg is in the dark.

22/09/00

James File

Hatton Garden Diamonds
22/09/00

Diamond 1.02 carats	£2,750.00
Paid	Lloyds Mcard
Mr J. Cameron	4775 9180 2227 4176 Exp. 12/00

Hackett Tailors
Sloane Street
London SW1
23/09/00

Tie	£45.00
Paid	Lloyds Mcard
Mr J. Cameron	4775 9180 2227 4176 Exp. 12/00

Nobu Restaurant
19 Old Park Lane
London W1
23/09/00

Meal	£185.00
Paid	Lloyds Mcard
Mr J. Cameron	4775 9180 2227 4176 Exp. 12/00
	Auth. 22.40

Even for him, James has been working very hard in the last few weeks. A lot of travel and a very full diary.

But he's been buying. The item from Hatton Garden Diamonds should catch anyone's eye. Not least Cynthia's. Just around a carat. Not a big flash stone, but single. And unset. He's taking the romantic route again. Bought the diamond loose and going to have it set, with the ring of her choice.

Imagine the scene. The restaurant. A small velveteen pouch, burning a hole in his pocket. When does he go for it? After the meal.

'Cynthia, darling. Would you . . .' No. 'Will you . . .'

One other sweet little detail. James bought himself a new tie that morning. Specially for the occasion.

25/09/00

<u>**James File**</u>

Le Pont de la Tour
Butlers Wharf
London SE1
25/09/00

Meal   £195.00

Paid   Lloyds Mcard
Mr J. Cameron   4775 9180 2227 4176   Exp. 12/00
                              Auth. 14.35

Tel. No. 020 7604 3490
81 Bryanston Road
London NW6 8KR

<u>Time</u>   <u>Number</u>   <u>Duration</u>
20.13   0131 225 1249   28.34 mins

James is not his usual sensible self. He's spending big on lunch. Takes a few of the mates out to Le Pont de la Tour. It's a big celebration for him.

I'd guess that Cynthia said yes.

Specially as James calls his mother that evening for a longish chat.

Meanwhile Cynths is keeping things low key. She had lunch out. But no steak this time. Just a little red wine.

And she doesn't call her folks that evening. The parents still don't know about the marriage plans.

10/10/00

James File

Cynthia File

The Times

OCTOBER 10TH 2000

MR JAMES CAMERON AND MS CYNTHIA SHEPHERD

The engagement is announced between James, son of the late Richard and Mrs Alice Cameron of Edinburgh, and Cynthia, daughter of Mr and Mrs Gerald Shepherd of Andover, Hampshire.

Tel. No. 020 7604 3490
81 Bryanston Road
London NW6 8KR

Time	Number	Duration
19.45	01264 332 365	14.01 mins

The announcement in the paper makes it official. James and Cynthia are engaged. Robert and Cynthia are having an affair. The triangle rips at the heart.

At last Cynths calls home.

She's made no big song and dance about things. Delayed calling her parents to tell them about the engagement until after the announcement. Doesn't feel like she's too happy with things. In two minds about which one to choose.

Why else did she get me to look into Robert and James?

To find out something crucial about one of them? Has to be. Maybe I missed something. One clue that didn't get cleared up.

12/10/00

James File

jamesc@aandersen.co.uk
Lotus Notes

12/10 20.00   Dinner Nico [Clients]

Robert File

Mobile Tel. No. 07962 783 411

Time	Number	Duration
10.15	020 7565 3466	3.20 mins
19.20	07694 297 614	1.58 mins
19.24	020 7565 3466	1.24 mins
19.26	020 7836 7243	2.55 mins

192.com
020 7565 3466   Nico
020 7836 7243   Mon Plaisir

James's office diary shows that he has a client dinner on Thursday 12th. The group is booked in at a restaurant called Nico. There are six in the party. All that's fine and dandy.

Until, on the morning of the twelfth, Robert rings Nico. He must be making a booking too. Again nothing too much to get excited about: Nico is a smart London restaurant – the sort of place that one would expect James and Robert to go to with clients. But when is Robert's reservation for? He books a cab for that evening through his secretary to take him from the office to an address in London W1 at 8.15. The address is Park Lane. Yeah, you've guessed it: Robert and James are going to be in the same restaurant at the same time. Where will Cynthia be? Has Robert booked an evening à *deux*, or does he have a business dinner too?

We shall know. We do know. At 7.20 Robert calls Cynthia on her mobile. At 7.24 he calls Nico. At 7.26 he calls another restaurant, Mon Plaisir.

He has changed the booking. He is having dinner with Cynthia. When he rang her there was a brief conversation that probably went along the lines of: 'I've booked a table at Nico for eight thirty.' 'Nico – we can't go to Nico, James is going there.' 'Christ, is he? OK, I'll change it. How about Mon Plaisir?' 'Fine. That was a close call.'

Could be that Cynthia only knew that James was going to Nico by chance. She knew he had a work dinner – that gave her the opportunity to meet up with Robert. Maybe he only mentioned Nico as he was leaving in the morning. She heard the name in half sleep: 'See you later, darling . . . have a nice evening . . .'

Robert pays for the meal at Mon Plaisir. VISA authorization time is 9.48. Cynthia is probably home by 10.20. She's there before James.

Robert File

Mon Plaisir
21 Monmouth Street
London WC2
12/10/00

Small Perrier	£2.75
1 Bt Hse Red	£15.75
1 Veg Millefeuille	£6.50
1 Escargot	£7.95
1 Boeuf Bourg	£12.95
Total	£45.90
Service @ 10%	£4.59
Total	£50.49

Paid   AMEX
Mr R. Bolton   3714 982416 3428   Exp. 02/01
                         Member since 1995
                         Auth. 21.48

That's how it goes: lies hidden by truth. Cynthia says she's meeting a girlfriend one night. If James were to suspect anything, she could prove who she was with and that they went to *Madame Bovary* together. Now when she does need to cover her tracks, he's not going to bother to worry. *She told the truth the last time, didn't she, why should I worry now?*

So she and Robert are free to have dinner together at Mon Plaisir while James is entertaining clients. Opportunity greeted and readily taken.

Sure, but take another look at the bill. One bottle of red wine; two starters, vegetable millefeuille and escargots; and only one main course, boeuf bourgignon. Cynthia eats steak; but the Dogg bets that weakness doesn't extend to beef casserole. So, Cynthia didn't have a main course. And they weren't at the restaurant all that late. Cynthia was either not feeling too good or off her appetite.

31/10/00

James File

jamesc@aandersen.co.uk
Lotus Notes

31/10	EuroDisney Conference
03/11	Return EuroDisney

Cynthia File

Cynthia Shepherd
MORI Diary

31/10	Out all day

Robert File

Robert Bolton
Saatchi & Saatchi Electronic Diary

31/10	Research [Do not phone]

Tel. No. 020 7635 0579
27 Cranleigh Gardens
London SW6 5TT

Time	Number	Duration
11.10	020 7394 2872	12.34 mins

Cynthia File

Mobile Tel. No. 07694 297 614

Time	Number	Duration
11.25	07962 783 411	3.20 mins

Metro Cabs
Saatchi & Saatchi Account No. 134

Account	Name	Destination	Time
612	N/A	81 Bryanston Rd, NW6 [pick-up 27 Cranleigh Gardens SW6]	18.30

Three weeks later. Cynthia and Robert are up to it again. They both take the day off work, I'd guess. Cynthia takes a taxi to his place that morning. She stays all day and returns home via cab around 6.30.

Probably told James she was going to spend the day with a girlfriend. Things are getting hotter. Our lovers are taking more risks.

01/11/00

<u>Cynthia File</u>

MediSearch . . . accessing files Dr Gavin Richardson . . .
patient: Ms C. Shepherd

Dr Gavin Richardson
01/11/00
Antenatal Appointment

Pregnant 15/40. O/E BP 110/70. Urine – no sugar, no protein. Fetal heart heard – sonic aid. See 4/52 midwife.

All well. Has had first booking appt. Dating scan compatible with dates. Nuchal fold low risk. First hospital appt next week with double test. Discussed patient concerns.

Note: bruises at wrists and ankles – says fell off bicycle.

Cynthia makes another appointment to see her GP. That evening. No real need for a second visit, unless there's a problem with the pregnancy and the doctor's notes don't suggest there is. So whatever she said, she had to have been going for another reason. Something is hurting.

And there's a hint: bruises at the wrists and ankles. Oh, come on, Cynth. Was it really a bicycle accident? I bet you don't even have a cycle. You just wanted to talk.

How's she going to explain the bruises to James? Maybe she doesn't have to. He's at a conference at EuroDisney for a few days. Accountants in Wonderland!

And while he's away – wounds heal.

02/11/00

Robert File

Mobile Tel. No. 07962 783 411

Time	Number	Duration
14.25	07694 297 614	0.07 mins
14.45	07694 297 614	0.05 mins
15.15	07694 297 614	0.09 mins
16.04	07694 297 614	4.04 mins

Tel. No. 020 7394 2872 x 271
MORI
95 Southwark Street
London SE1

Time	Number	Duration
16.10	0777 242 1649	4.20 mins

The following morning Robert calls Cynthia on her mobile. Six times. She only answers the first call and then only speaks for 2.40 minutes. She doesn't want to speak to Robert.

Robert keeps calling Cynthia that afternoon. Looks like he puts down the moment he gets put through to her voice-mail. She answers the fourth call. They speak for 4.04 minutes.

Cynthia then calls James. They speak for some four minutes too.

07/11/00 status

thedogg@acdogg.co.uk
Visitor file:
cynths@mori.org   on-line 17 mins

Still getting those 'track that bastard husband of mine' e-mail requests. Thanks again for the publicity, Cynth.

But one visitor to my site acted kind of strange. Stayed for seventeen minutes. Well, that's neighbourly of them, but there's not a lot to see. Only one page.

So why stay so long and not say anything? Not leave me a message? Of course you could have just forgotten that you were logged on. Or did you want to say something but couldn't? Did you want to ask for my help but then backed off?

My instinct twitches. Feels like this girl comes to my office. She stands outside the door. I can see her through the plate glass. I can almost smell her perfume. It's Allure.

Is this the moment? Do I cross over? Do I open the door? Do I send an anonymous message to the police? 'The Yard' would never get the plot. Got to stick to the case and stick to the girl.

08/11/00

<u>Cynthia File</u>

TeleTaxis
MORI Account

<u>Name</u>	<u>Destination</u>	<u>Time</u>
Ms C. Shepherd	Cranleigh Gardens SW6	19.00

Tel. No. 020 7635 0579
27 Cranleigh Gardens
London SW6 5TT

<u>Time</u>	<u>Number</u>	<u>Duration</u>
20.23	020 7604 3940	0.34 mins
20.26	0777 242 1649	0.23 mins

It is November 8th. In the evening Cynthia takes another cab to Robert's house in Cranleigh Gardens, Fulham. Just a few doors down from where her rapist lives. She does not know this – maybe they bumped into one another.

The cab arrives at 7.48.

There's a telephone call from Robert's flat at 8.23. It's to James and Cynthia's number. No answer. Another call to James's mobile phone at 8.26. No reply. James is out – maybe another business meeting?

After that there are no more calls.

08/11/00

Cynthia File

Tel. No. 020 7604 3940
81 Bryanston Road
London NW6 8KR

Time	Number	Duration
21.32	01264 332369	10.01 mins
21.45	020 7485 0763	4.45 mins

192.com

Domino's Pizzas   020 7485 0763

Domino's Pizzas
Most Frequently Ordered
   Pizza   Quattro Stagioni
Ave. Delivery Time   26 mins
08/11/00

1 x Vegetariana	£9.50
1 x Peroni Beer	£2.50
1 x Green Salad	£3.00
Total	£15.00

Delivery Address   Garden Flat, 81 Bryanston Road, NW6

Paid   VISA
Ms C. Shepherd   4550 9698 1291 7461   Exp. 03/01
                         Auth. 21.48

Cynthia arrives home by 9.32; we know because she calls her mother at that time. She uses her credit card to order a takeaway pizza for one from Domino's Pizzas at 9.45. James must still be out; either that or he has already eaten.

09/11/00 12.05

LONDON WEATHER

Sunny
Temperature 12°

Robert File

Robert Bolton
Saatchi & Saatchi Electronic Diary

09/11 9.00–12.30   IKEA Final Presentation

Tel. No. 020 7511 1642
Saatchi & Saatchi
Charlotte Street
London W1

Time	Number	Duration
9.45	07962 783 411	1.32 mins
10.31	020 7635 0579	1.45 mins
10.50	020 7635 0579	0.09 mins
11.20	07962 783 411	0.45 mins
11.28	020 7734 6969	12.56 mins

Metropolitan Police Report

WORKING FOR A SAFER LONDON

Incident No. 46474: Attend 27 Cranleigh Gardens SW6. Male found dead.

Initial Coroner's Report

Cause of death: drugs overdose. Time of death: 22.00–24.00 hrs on 08/11/00.

The following morning breaks on London. It's a bright, mild day.

Robert's secretary makes four calls: to Robert's mobile then to his home flat. No answer at either.

Then at 11.28 a director at Robert's office calls the Fulham police. He has not been in to work, and has not returned his secretary's calls. It is all very out of character. Could they check his flat?

The police attend 27 Cranleigh Gardens at 15.39.

Robert is found dead in a chair. He has been dead for some time. A subsequent post-mortem suggests time of death somewhere between ten and midnight the previous evening. He died from a drugs overdose.

13/11/00 15.40

<u>Robert File</u>

Robert Bolton

Credit cards   Mastercard Gold Card
                      4323 7004 6110 9754
                      Barclays VISA Card
                      4929 8112 7430 6139
                      American Express Corporate
                      3714 982416 3428

Accounts closed.

Robert in the morgue. More sadness. More silent screams. Robert, you dumb idiot, why make such a stupid mistake? Did you push it too far just one more time? Take a risk, again? Maybe you were no saint. No-one is. Earth's not the right place for saints. You misled your best friend, you bedded his girl. And you probably even deceived her – bet you didn't tell her about the file I sent you. But it's not for me to judge you about that. I'd be making assumptions. And what's more, I don't have a reason. I don't have a motive. All I have is what I read from the screen. That's the only way I get to experience things. I learn without the experience. And that's how I keep objective. Even about death.

Mortality. We are 'soft sift in an hour glass'. We are also soft data. A bundle of messages made flesh. We are soft ware.

I am soft ware. I can cope with it. But can you? Or do you think you're so individual, so immortal – so human?

Or are we hard facts? Evidence on the trail. The different sides of existence: soft ware, hard facts. The soul is bared on the road taken.

Life's reduced to banal graffiti:

> To be is to do.
> To do is to be.

From this is derived 'The Dogg's Law of Circularity': Be = Do.
Let's hum it.
Do be do be do.
Frank Sinatra got it right. 'Strangers in the Night'.

Robert File

Metropolitan Police Report

WORKING FOR A SAFER LONDON

Case No. 46474
Robert Bolton
27 Cranleigh Gardens, SW6
Death by drugs overdose
DC Richards No. 323990

Search Items: diaries, letters, photographs. Link to Case No. File JettisonA 24355 8890.
Ms Anita Jettison: death from drugs overdose 26/05/00

> Interview:
> Ms Anthea Sims [secretary]
> Mr B. Cartwright [friend]
> Ms C. Shepherd [friend. Note: Ms C. Shepherd, Garden Flat, 81 Bryanston Road,
>   NW6. Length of interview 34 minutes]
> Mr B. Thompkins [neighbour]

Case closed.

Coroner's Report

Death by drugs overdose. Accidental Death.

How did Robert die? An overdose. The coroner doesn't appear to have seen cause for suspicion. The coroner's officers carry out routine investigations. But they do interview Cynthia. They question her for nearly forty minutes, according to the file. Then no more contact.

Robert could have committed suicide. It wouldn't have been entirely out of character. But again, it's not something we would have expected. It was just a sick, sad mistake. Though I have to say the police report makes interesting reading for the Dogg. First, it vindicates the Dogg's own findings. The police find a link; they connect Robert to Anita's death. There were photographs in his flat of Anita, signed 'With love, A'. There was also a whole bundle of newspaper cuttings about her death. And loads of drugs. Finally there were his diaries. The report cites various entries relating to Anita's death; maybe he did the same thing? 'To be or not to be' stuff everywhere. Robert clearly felt he was to blame.

There was no mention of my Cynthia file. They probably didn't have the wit to check out Robert's hard drive.

The report's filed; the coroner's drawn his conclusion: no-one else was involved. Accidental Death – with the probable inference that he took his own life in remorse, blaming himself for Anita's death.

So it is: we shall not know exactly how Robert died. Like Anita's death, it will remain a mystery. There is an end to all our knowing. Cynthia appears innocent, even though she was probably the last person to see him alive. The report files show she told the police that Robert was an old friend. He had called her earlier that day complaining that he was feeling very depressed. He needed someone to talk to and as a friend she had felt a responsibility to go and see him. When she arrived he had been rather drunk and was taking drugs; she stayed for about half an hour. They talked about his problems. She told the police he was afraid he was going to get the sack from Saatchis' and, combined with his lack of funds, this was putting him under huge pressure. She had left feeling that he was depressed and unhappy, but she had never dreamt that he would do anything silly. In fact, he had perked up considerably while she was there. So she felt fine about leaving him and going home.

23/11/00   19.25

<u>**Cynthia File**</u>

Counselling and Psychotherapy Partnership
23/11/00

Appt 2.00–2.50   £110.00

Paid   VISA
Ms C. Shepherd   4550 9698 1291 7461   Exp. 03/01

Still looking for the answer, Cynthia?

Is that really how it went with Robert? Or did you talk about your child? Did you tell Robert that it could be his baby? Did he threaten to ring James? Did you tell him it frightened you to be tied up, and did you remember what I said? Someone tried to ring James that day. From a call box. Maybe it was Robert trying to get through to James that evening, not you. He was going to tell James about your affair. The Dogg returns to the question: did Robert really commit suicide?

Answer, it depends on when you stop looking for the answer. All data depends on when. Right now, the case is uncertain. Maybe Cynthia is telling the truth. The truth, that is, as she remembers it, or even the truth that she has convinced herself of. Lies become fact in the internal world, if you tell them to yourself hard enough and long enough. The picture gets distorted in recollection. That's why the Dogg sticks to the facts. The only way to proceed in this uncertain world. But knowledge is a dangerous thing. The tree bears poison fruit. The innocent do not search. The wise know when to stop searching. The Dogg keeps on.

All we can say for certain is Roberto is dead. Departed and gone. Fact.

02/12/00

James File

Cynthia File

LONDON WEATHER

Sunny
Temperature 13º

CAMDEN REGISTER OFFICE

11.30   Mr J. Cameron & Ms C. Shepherd

You are beginning to dream good dreams . . .

So here we are at the Register Office watching happy couples get hitched.

There is now one more to add to the list.

James and Cynthia Cameron. My two protégés are getting married. They will be happy. A child is on the way. Life will be sweet and straightforward. The Dogg bets they will stay together. Love's story, that's what we really have here. Two people who do love one another, though they may ignore it, or mistreat it, or even deny it. In the end, it's 'stand by me'.

And the Dogg? I must go on about a Dogg's business.

The Dogg continues, will not relent. I am the Dogg. Alone.

09/12/00   12.00

James File

File Cam2455: James Cameron
Dr S. Faversham
182 Harley Street
London W1N 2AP

update 14/09/00
Lab Test No. 234677 – Harley Street Centre

– less than 3.7 million/ml
– 21 %
– 76 % abnormal

Diagnosis: severe oligoasthenoteratozoospermia. Very low possibility of fertility.

BP 24 Hour
96 Cranleigh Gardens
London SW6
08/11/00

17 Litres Super-unleaded	£24.03
1 Cigarettes – 10 Marlboro Lights	£2.12
1 Matches	£0.10
Total	£26.25

Paid   Lloyds Mcard
Mr J. Cameron   4775 9180 2227 4176   Exp. 12/00
                              Auth. 22.45

The end of a little love story. It has all worked out for two people. Men and women are better together than alone. Alone you ain't got no chance of a happy ending.

That's why I didn't say anything. You know, at that bit in the wedding when someone asks whether there is anyone who knows of any 'just cause or impediment'. I could have said something then. After all, we're all in the congregation now. It's an on-line world, so everyone's a witness.

I didn't say a word: didn't cross the line. Though a couple of late items on the file did come to mind.

Remember James's visit to Dr Faversham in Harley Street? The Dogg has finally tracked the file through to the lab which carried out the tests. He is almost certainly infertile.

Oh, and by the way.

James bought seventeen litres of unleaded petrol and a packet of ten Marlboro Lights. In a twenty-four-hour petrol station. At the corner of Cranleigh Gardens. At 10.45 p.m. on November 8th. The night that Robert died.

I didn't tell. That's the choice I made, Cynthia. But am I right?

Privacy girl, you asked, 'How much should we know about each other?' You argued that we own our own data. You want to set limits on what we know.

But should I tell you what I know about James? Do you want to know that he is not the father of your child? Do you want to know he knows that? Do you want to know he was there the night Robert died?

Cynths, how much do you want to know?

You know where I am.